The Toughest Ranger

SELECTED FICTION WORKS BY L. RON HUBBARD

FANTASY

The Case of the Friendly Corpse

Death's Deputy

Fear

The Ghoul

The Indigestible Triton

Slaves of Sleep & The Masters of Sleep

Typewriter in the Sky

The Ultimate Adventure

SCIENCE FICTION

Battlefield Earth

The Conquest of Space

The End Is Not Yet

Final Blackout

The Kilkenny Cats

The Kingslayer

The Mission Earth Dekalogy*

Ole Doc Methuselah

To the Stars

ADVENTURE

The Hell Job series

WESTERN

Buckskin Brigades

Empty Saddles

Guns of Mark Jardine

Hot Lead Payoff

A full list of L. Ron Hubbard's
novellas and short stories is provided at the back.

*Dekalogy—a group of ten volumes

L. RON HUBBARD

The Toughest Ranger

Published by
Galaxy Press, LLC
7051 Hollywood Boulevard, Suite 200
Hollywood, CA 90028

Printed in the United States of America.

ISBN-10 1-59212-375-9
ISBN-13 978-1-59212-375-9

Library of Congress Control Number: 2007903537

Contents

FOREWORD

Stories from Pulp Fiction's Golden Age

AND it *was* a golden age.

The 1930s and 1940s were a vibrant, seminal time for a gigantic audience of eager readers, probably the largest per capita audience of readers in American history. The magazine racks were chock-full of publications with ragged trims, garish cover art, cheap brown pulp paper, low cover prices—and the most excitement you could hold in your hands.

"Pulp" magazines, named for their rough-cut, pulpwood paper, were a vehicle for more amazing tales than Scheherazade could have told in a million and one nights. Set apart from higher-class "slick" magazines, printed on fancy glossy paper with quality artwork and superior production values, the pulps were for the "rest of us," adventure story after adventure story for people who liked to *read.* Pulp fiction authors were no-holds-barred entertainers—real storytellers. They were more interested in a thrilling plot twist, a horrific villain or a white-knuckle adventure than they were in lavish prose or convoluted metaphors.

The sheer volume of tales released during this wondrous golden age remains unmatched in any other period of literary history—hundreds of thousands of published stories in over nine hundred different magazines. Some titles lasted only an issue or two; many magazines succumbed to paper shortages during World War II, while others endured for decades yet. Pulp fiction remains as a treasure trove of stories you can read, stories you can love, stories you can remember. The stories were driven by plot and character, with grand heroes, terrible villains, beautiful damsels (often in distress), diabolical plots, amazing places, breathless romances. The readers wanted to be taken beyond the mundane, to live adventures far removed from their ordinary lives—and the pulps rarely failed to deliver.

In that regard, pulp fiction stands in the tradition of all memorable literature. For as history has shown, good stories are much more than fancy prose. William Shakespeare, Charles Dickens, Jules Verne, Alexandre Dumas—many of the greatest literary figures wrote their fiction for the readers, not simply literary colleagues and academic admirers. And writers for pulp magazines were no exception. These publications reached an audience that dwarfed the circulations of today's short story magazines. Issues of the pulps were scooped up and read by over thirty million avid readers each month.

Because pulp fiction writers were often paid no more than a cent a word, they had to become prolific or starve. They also had to write aggressively. As Richard Kyle, publisher and editor of *Argosy,* the first and most long-lived of the pulps, so pointedly explained: "The pulp magazine writers, the best of them, worked for markets that did not write for critics or attempt to satisfy timid advertisers. Not having to answer to anyone other than their readers, they wrote about human beings on the edges of the unknown, in those new lands the future would explore. They wrote for what we would become, not for what we had already been."

Some of the more lasting names that graced the pulps include H. P. Lovecraft, Edgar Rice Burroughs, Robert E. Howard, Max Brand, Louis L'Amour, Elmore Leonard, Dashiell Hammett, Raymond Chandler, Erle Stanley Gardner, John D. MacDonald, Ray Bradbury, Isaac Asimov, Robert Heinlein—and, of course, L. Ron Hubbard.

In a word, he was among the most prolific and popular writers of the era. He was also the most enduring—hence this series—and certainly among the most legendary. It all began only months after he first tried his hand at fiction, with L. Ron Hubbard tales appearing in *Thrilling Adventures, Argosy, Five-Novels Monthly, Detective Fiction Weekly, Top-Notch, Texas Ranger, War Birds, Western Stories,* even *Romantic Range.* He could write on any subject, in any genre, from jungle explorers to deep-sea divers, from G-men and gangsters, cowboys and flying aces to mountain climbers, hard-boiled detectives and spies. But he really began to shine when he turned his talent to science fiction and fantasy of which he authored nearly fifty novels or novelettes to forever change the shape of those genres.

Following in the tradition of such famed authors as Herman Melville, Mark Twain, Jack London and Ernest Hemingway, Ron Hubbard actually lived adventures that his own characters would have admired—as an ethnologist among primitive tribes, as prospector and engineer in hostile climes, as a captain of vessels on four oceans. He even wrote a series of articles for *Argosy,* called "Hell Job," in which he lived and told of the most dangerous professions a man could put his hand to.

Finally, and just for good measure, he was also an accomplished photographer, artist, filmmaker, musician and educator. But he was first and foremost a *writer,* and that's the L. Ron Hubbard we come to know through the pages of this volume.

This library of Stories from the Golden Age presents the best of L. Ron Hubbard's fiction from the heyday of storytelling, the Golden Age of the pulp magazines. In these eighty volumes, readers are treated to a full banquet of 153 stories, a kaleidoscope of tales representing every imaginable genre: science fiction, fantasy, western, mystery, thriller, horror, even romance—action of all kinds and in all places.

Because the pulps themselves were printed on such inexpensive paper with high acid content, issues were not meant to endure. As the years go by, the original issues of every pulp from *Argosy* through *Zeppelin Stories* continue crumbling into brittle, brown dust. This library preserves the L. Ron Hubbard tales from that era, presented with a distinctive look that brings back the nostalgic flavor of those times.

L. Ron Hubbard's Stories from the Golden Age has something for every taste, every reader. These tales will return you to a time when fiction was good clean entertainment and the most fun a kid could have on a rainy afternoon or the best thing an adult could enjoy after a long day at work.

Pick up a volume, and remember what reading is supposed to be all about. Remember curling up with a *great story.*

—Kevin J. Anderson

KEVIN J. ANDERSON *is the author of more than ninety critically acclaimed works of speculative fiction, including The Saga of Seven Suns, the continuation of the Dune Chronicles with Brian Herbert, and his* New York Times *bestselling novelization of L. Ron Hubbard's* Ai! Pedrito!

The Toughest Ranger

Chapter One

THE Arizona sun beat pitilessly down upon the dun plain and warped and baked the tired trees which drooped about the 'dobe ranch house.

The road, little more than two wagon tracks, started in a joined point on one horizon and ended in another point at the western limit of the plain. It was endless, that road, endless and dry and hot. And down it came Petey McGuire, leading his horse, the little sorrel named Pat.

Petey McGuire's high heels were run over; his Stetson was shapeless; his jeans were worn through at the knees. About his waist hung suspended from scraped leather an old Peacemaker. His young face was haggard and coated with a pasty mixture of dust and sweat. His eyes were hopeless.

Pat, with lowered head, limped after him. The little sorrel's flanks were white with dried lather, his coat was roughened and spotted with cockleburs. It was all he could do to keep going, but keep going he did as long as his nose was close against Petey McGuire's back.

Pat had thrown a shoe and Pat had spent himself on a journey of a thousand miles and Pat, oatless these many weeks, was a dead horse unless he got rest and care.

Shuffling with weariness, slogging through the dust, they came to the ranch house gate just as a thickset fellow rode out.

It was endless, that road, endless and dry and hot.
And down it came Petey McGuire, leading his horse,
the little sorrel named Pat.

The stranger would have ridden straight by if Petey had not stopped him. But Petey did with a pleading gesture.

"Mister," said Petey looking wistfully up, "I got to have a job. I got to get Pat shoed and get some oats into him before . . ."

"Not hiring anybody—like you," said the stranger.

Petey blinked and felt anger redden his face. "We need some rest, that's all. I can punch cows. I thought this newer country would be better than Kansas. . . ."

"It ain't a question of punchin' cows," said the stranger curtly. "It's a question of punchin' rustlers. What I need is fightin' men." With a flick of his quirt the ranch owner sent his mount forward and the abruptness of his departure was an insult.

"Saddle tramp," Petey told Pat. "That's all I am. A saddle tramp." With a surge of rage, he said, "Damn him. How the hell does he know I can't fight? How . . ."

Pat was standing with his left ear forward, listening though he could not hold up his tired head.

"He's right," said Petey. "Yeah. He's right. What do I know about fightin'? Yeah. Just a kid, just nobody. No jobs for kids, Pat. No jobs for a guy that can't spit smoke."

He led onward at a slower, more hopeless gait than before. He walked for a mile or more and then stopped again.

"Hell," said Petey McGuire.

It was a doleful word, a substitute for a woman's tears.

He started on again with Pat slogging after him.

Mile after mile, mile after mile, and above, the scorching sun hammered molten arrows into Petey's back, made the brass saddle horn too hot to touch. But he would not ride. He would not further abuse the only friend he had.

The world could find no use for Petey McGuire. He was too young. He was not tough enough. He had soft blue eyes and red cheeks and though he was of medium height he did not give the impression of being tall.

On the run from Kansas. On the run for a thousand miles. In Kansas a foreman had thrashed him thoroughly, had pushed his face into the mud just because Petey had spoken up to say . . .

But, hell, what did it matter? What did anything matter? Wasn't he always running away? Wasn't he always slogging over leagues of the West, from starvation to starvation interspersed with jobs he never kept?

On the run from a father who had been something less than kind. On the run from a beating he still winced to remember. And now at twenty-four he was still on the run. Job to job, beating to beating.

"Yeah," said Petey McGuire with bitter inflection. "Yeah. Saddle tramp."

He'd like to kill them. All of them. The foreman who had thrashed him, the endless others who had plagued him. The punchers who had jeered at him for silky blond hair and soft blue eyes.

And always the reason had been the same. Always he had been too soft. He had roped a calf and his Pat had slipped upon the muddy plain, and before he could loosen up the rope, the calf had died. And he had not been able to keep back tears.

The foreman had been about to shoot a horse and Petey, yelling in sudden rage, although the broken leg . . .

"Yeah, saddle tramp," muttered Petey McGuire.

He had taught Pat tricks, clever tricks and when punchers had laughed at him because he talked to Pat and told him dreams . . . Yes. Sure. He had cried.

"Saddle tramp," muttered Petey McGuire.

He was too softhearted, that was all. He couldn't stand to see men and beasts suffer. He couldn't stand jeers.

But now it was strange the way the sun affected him. His mouth was curled down in a bitter grimace. He'd like to kill them, every one. Just because they thought a man was less a man because he felt things more deeply, he was on the run. Over leagues of the West. From Kansas to Arizona.

They didn't call him Petey. They called him "Sweetheart" and "Mary."

This feeling within him was strange. Before he had tried to excuse them but now . . . Now he wanted to kill them for what they had done to him for twenty-four years. And now poor Pat was getting the backslap of it. Pat needed oats and bright shoes and a cool stall.

That stranger's remark had done an odd thing to him. He had wanted to whip up the Peacemaker and shoot—shoot with cold and awful accuracy and bring that heavy fool down into the dirt with blood pouring from his head.

Petey felt the surprise of feeling such a thing. It was foreign to him. He was no fighting man and the stranger knew it well by the slightest glance.

But never before had Petey felt this helpless, blind rage against the world which wouldn't have him in it, the world which drove him on, the world which was now trying to kill Pat.

He did not know how far he went as his legs were numb and walking, mechanical. But when he looked up he was on the outskirts of a small pueblo. The biggest building in it was a fort-like 'dobe structure which presented an arched gate to the road. There was a sign about that gate: "THE ARIZONA RANGERS."

Petey stopped, hardly seeing the sign at all. In this town, he knew, he could swab out a bar for food. He could clean up a stable. . . .

But Pat had to have shoes and oats and a few weeks' rest.

He turned and looked at the weary little cow pony who didn't even raise his head. Pat pushed ahead a staggering step and shoved his muzzle into Petey's chest.

"Yeah," said Petey. "Yeah. I know. I'm hungry too."

He went toward a saloon and wrapped Pat's reins about the hitchrack. Petey stepped through the doors and into the dim interior.

The bartender was a thick-jowled fellow, shining up glasses. He took one look at Petey and marked him for what he was—saddle tramp.

"Beat it," said the bartender before Petey had spoken. "We got a swamper. There ain't no room in Cristobal for saddle tramps."

"Look," pleaded Petey.

"Yeah, but you better do the lookin'. Captain Shannon

locks up every man that can't pay his way. He's cleanin' up the country, see? He's tough, the toughest Ranger in the state and you better take my tip. Beat it."

"You mean . . . you mean just because I'm broke he'd lock me up?" said Petey.

"Well? Why not?"

A chill of terror shook Petey. He turned around and went out into the street. He stopped with Pat's reins in his hand and stared at the big 'dobe building which was marked with the sign: "THE ARIZONA RANGERS."

He knew what he faced. If they locked him up, Pat . . . He hadn't realized until now how shabby Pat looked after a thousand miles. They wouldn't take care of Pat.

But he couldn't go on. No, he couldn't take to the desert again. That way lay death. And here was death for Pat.

His hand was shaking as he pulled his hat brim down. He had no solution for this. Captain Shannon was tough, toughest Ranger in the state. . . .

Petey swallowed hard.

If Pat . . .

Suddenly he wanted to hit somebody, anybody. He wanted to lash out and slay these ghosts which had stalked him for twenty-four years. His rage began to mount.

They had no right to do this to him. No right to kill Pat by loosing him on the waterless desert. Pat needed care!

Suddenly Petey McGuire felt cold. His wits felt like crystal in his head. He was not shaking. He had felt himself grow taller and the experience did not even surprise him. His young face was set and his blue eyes were suddenly hard.

They couldn't kill Pat.

And he knew what he could do.

It was an amazingly brazen idea.

Without any volition of his own he found himself leading Pat across the road and to the 'dobe fort's gate.

Petey was without any fear of anything. He was five times bigger than the sentry.

Maybe it was the sun. Maybe it was starvation. Maybe it was the thought of losing his only friend.

But Petey snapped at the leather-faced sentry, "Where's Shannon?"

He did not recognize his own voice.

The sentry jerked his thumb toward another archway within. Petey, leading Pat, went toward it.

He could see a man beyond. That must be Shannon. A granite boulder behind a desk.

Half of Petey was suddenly scared to death. But the other half of him would not stop walking. He dropped Pat's reins and stalked into the office with a careless, impudent swagger.

Captain Shannon looked up, annoyed, starting to stamp the caller by his dusty, torn clothing.

But Petey was without fear now. Nothing could stop Petey. Not even himself.

"M'name's McGuire," said Petey in a challenging tone. "Petey McGuire. You've heard of me."

Shannon started to make a biting remark, but Petey rushed on without any help from Petey.

"Petey McGuire. From Kansas City to N'Orleans, what I say goes. I'm so tough I'd give a rattler nightmares. You're

Shannon and I hear you need tough guys. Well, you ain't got anybody around here that'd stand up to me."

"I don't think . . ." began Shannon sarcastically.

"Hell! You trying to tell me you never heard of Petey McGuire? G'wan, I ain't in no mood for telling funny stories. Where's my badge and where's my bunk? And don't take all day about it!"

Petey was scared down. He was so scared he expected Shannon to leap at him across that battered desk.

But Shannon looked at a dusty, hard-faced, reckless fellow with a twisted grin on his mouth and a swagger in the way he stood.

Shannon was taken not a little aback. He knew his own reputation and now that he was getting old he was guarding it. He had reasons. He had made enemies in his day. And this tough-talking kid had more brass than anybody Shannon had seen for many a year. Shannon's reputation was such as to demand respect. And here was a young whippersnapper . . .

Shannon got up and came around the desk. He was taller than Petey by half a foot and heavier by fifty pounds.

With malice, Shannon said, "So you're tough, are you, sonny?"

Petey startled himself by bristling, "The name's McGuire. Petey McGuire, and if you ain't heard of me you don't know nothin'. Where's the badge and the bunk?"

Shannon scratched his jaw and squinted up a cold, gray eye. He was amused. But now was not the time. Oh, no. He could read this kid like a book. Youngster putting on a front and nothing more and when the guns began to go . . .

Shannon had a sense of humor.

"Hunter will show you the bunk. We'll see about you later."

Petey found that he was going out of the door. He went up to Pat and blindly bumped into something white beside the pony. Petey discovered it was a girl.

But the role which had dropped over him like a coat of mail would not desert him now. Some evil devil had slid down out of the blue, had leaped into mild Petey McGuire and was now bent upon his destruction.

"Look where you're goin'!" said Petey.

The girl was astonished. She was a little thing, perhaps twenty, and she was fragilely beautiful. Her lovely gray eyes were wide as she backed up.

"I . . . I'm sorry," she stammered. "I was looking at the pony. He's been ridden very hard."

"Yeah," snapped Petey.

And she did something she had never done before in her life. She flashed, "You ought to be ashamed of yourself, killing a horse that way!"

"Blah!" said the devil inside Petey McGuire.

She backed up again and he surlily led Pat toward her so that she had to step out of the way again.

She was tight-lipped with fury at such insolence but he gave her not another glance.

Hunter came out of the barracks and saw him and fell in to show him to the stables.

And back in the office doorway, Captain Shannon looked bleakly at the departing rider and mount and then back at his daughter Bette.

She flashed, "You ought to be ashamed of yourself, killing a horse that way!"

Shannon's reputation was great. He had one thing in this world which was worth having, one thing which he protected so fiercely that the object itself was stricken with awe of him.

He looked at his daughter Bette and then back at the vanishing McGuire.

Bette walked toward the office, slowly, not seeing.

"Well?" said Shannon.

She gave a start.

"Never mind," said Shannon. "I'll get him for that."

"Oh no!" said Bette swiftly. "No. He was tired. I told him . . ."

She was stopped by the searching stare which her father gave her.

Guiltily she turned and walked down the veranda and when she turned a little to see if McGuire was still in sight, Shannon was still staring at her.

Chapter Two

TEN days later, the demon still possessed Petey McGuire. At least it seemed to him that something had dived from the fiery furnace into his soul. He had been very shaky at first. The range-toughened Rangers had tried to put him to the test with the jesting any new recruit will get.

And Petey McGuire had looked them in the eye while half of him stood back watching Petey McGuire look them in the eye. It was a puzzling thing.

The Rangers were courteous. And that was a new experience to Petey. He had looked them in the eye and had told them to go to hell and now they nodded to him pleasantly and stayed clear of him generally.

Respect was a new thing to him. It made him feel more than a little drunk. He swaggered around the barracks and compound, ever watchful and swiftly overbearing if any man crossed him.

Petey mulled the matter as he swabbed down Pat. Here he was, feeling a fairly normal Petey McGuire, but if anybody stepped up to him he knew he would give him a brisk snap. He was McGuire but he wasn't McGuire and never before in his life had he suspected his own double identity. He had been most busy dodging fights and now he had learned that if he kept up his front the fights would begin to dodge him.

He had only reached a solution to his past misery, but the force of it and the exhilaration of having people think he was tough evaded his personal discovery. He only knew that a demon had come along and that the demon had leaped into Petey McGuire and that he was sharing his house with a hellion.

He tried, now and then, to back down but he couldn't. The demon wouldn't let him.

"Funny," he told Pat. "If I didn't know this was me I'd think it was somebody else!"

Pat turned his head and bent his ears forward and looked at Petey and Petey stopped swabbing his pony.

"By God," said Petey, "you've changed too!"

It was oats that had done it. Oats and new, bright shoes. Pat's sorrel coat shimmered silkily and he carried his head high.

Petey had also done a bit of changing. Discarded were his tattered clothes. He had dragged on his pay for new jeans, brass-studded batwings, stiff, flat-brimmed Stetson and shiny boots. He had drawn a new Colt from the arsenal and he had polished it so much that the sun hitting it blinded a man.

With good food inside him and good clothes on him and with everybody in Cristobal half-believing he was a dangerous customer, Petey felt so good inside that he radiated confidence. His blue eyes were alert and his blond hair was carefully combed and, all in all, he looked about twice as Rangerish as a Ranger.

Now and then a traitorous thought hit Petey. One of these days somebody was going to call his bluff and then . . . then he didn't know whether he could deliver or not. That worried him not a little.

He became aware of an audience and turned to see Bette Shannon standing on a runway under the wall watching him.

She had a wide-brimmed hat on her head with a broad leather thong under her chin and the effect made her face smaller than ever, made her eyes bigger and grayer.

Evidently she had something to say but she was having a hard time getting enough courage to approach and talk. Her father discouraged her speaking to the men and since her mother had died eleven years before, only a few Mexican women had served as an outlet for conversation.

Petey unnecessarily began to make a checkerboard pattern on Pat's rump with his currycomb. After a while he knew that Bette Shannon was standing about five feet behind him as her slim shadow barely touched Petey's own.

Petey was in the grip of a devil. He couldn't help himself. Suddenly he was very bold and his grin was insolence itself. He turned cockily about and said, "Well?" His other half blinked in amazement. The old Petey usually got struck dumb in the presence of good women.

She was confused and blushed a little, nervously twisting at the chin thong's concha. "I . . . I'm sorry what I said, Mr. McGuire. I . . . you . . . your horse . . . You've done nothing but take care of him for ten days . . . that and shoot at a target. I . . . I was wrong, I guess, about you riding your horse on purpose that way and . . . and almost killing him."

"Yeah," said Petey. "I'm glad you found out you were wrong."

The old Petey drew a long breath and the new Petey grinned and said, "I may have buried a lot of men in my time, but I don't kill horses. Them as says Petey McGuire is tough also knows that Petey McGuire is kind to animals. I don't hold it against you. Any woman is going to be wrong once in a while."

Suddenly she was very austere. "You like yourself, don't you?"

This was a blow to the old Petey and he countered swiftly by wanting to be humble and beg her pardon and tell her, oh how badly, that he . . . But the new Petey said, "Sure. I'm good and I know I'm good. What's wrong with that?"

She walked away from him and he watched her go. The old Petey wanted to call her back or run after her and the new Petey just stood still and admired the way her riding skirt swung from side to side.

"What the hell did I do that for?" Petey demanded of Pat.

Pat looked at him and the sun got in his eye and he winked.

A new shadow fell across Petey's shoulder.

"Still tough?" said Shannon.

Petey whirled and looked up at the granite visage of the man. There was something horribly impersonal in Captain Shannon just as though he could shoot a fellow down and read a sermon without giving the matter another thought. The man was all gray, all cold. Hitting him would be like trying to knock over a mountain.

"Yeah," said Petey.

"And still cocky," said Shannon. "Look here, McGuire, I let you in on the chance that you might be half as good as you say you are. . . ."

"I'm better," said Petey.

"Yes? Be that as it may, youngster, but there's an unwritten rule around here that men take off their hats and say 'Yes, ma'am to Miss Shannon."

"Yeah?" said Petey.

"Yes," said Shannon. "And when Miss Shannon is around, men are not supposed to flirt with her and then try to insult her. Is that clear?"

"Yeah," said Petey.

"And hereafter," said Shannon, "you are not to talk to Miss Shannon."

"And if I do?" challenged the new Petey.

"You'll have me to deal with, McGuire."

The old Petey's shocked ears heard him laughing cynically at Shannon.

Shannon froze and his gray eyes froze and the old Petey froze, but the new Petey went on laughing.

"Shut up!" said Shannon. "You're nothing but a damned cocky kid. You don't know enough to be scared of anything. You've been burning up ammunition in practice and now you're going to have your chance to burn it up in earnest."

Shannon had not thought he would say this, but here he was saying it. Petey infuriated him beyond endurance.

"We haven't got time to lie around," snapped Shannon. "The cattlemen are howling for us to take rustlers out of business before the rustlers take the cattlemen out of business. Most of this troop is out now. All right, Mr. Jehovah McGuire, I got news two hours ago that Brad Thompson is in Grande Piedras. If you're so tough, go get him!"

The old Petey's knees began to knock. Thompson was a

gunman of the Shannon caliber. But the new Petey spoke up, "Sure. Nothing to it! I don't even want help and I'll have him back here at sundown."

He turned his back on Shannon and reached up to take Pat's saddle from its peg.

Shannon looked at Petey's squared back with slight misgivings. His rage had vanished before astonishment, but he showed none of it on his expressionless face.

Maybe this kid wasn't a bluff after all!

Chapter Three

GRANDE PIEDRAS was a collection of 'dobe huts along one bank of a river which contained more blue boulders than water. There was an old Jesuit church and a plaza around it and around the plaza squatted a long string of gambling houses and saloons as though picketing the House of God.

No priest had set foot in Grande Piedras for a century. The Jesuits had been recalled to Spain and the Franciscans had thought the town impossible to save.

It was a stone's throw from the border and here were assembled most of the gentlemen who did an uncomfortable business in other people's beef.

The sun was hot and men dozed in the shade and a Mexican plunked wearily and hopelessly under a balcony. The sound of his guitar and the buzz of flies and the far-off whir of a wheel told Petey that at least somebody was alive in the place.

He felt pretty small on Pat's back but he looked most competent and belligerent. He had fought a battle with himself about unpinning the Ranger's star from his vest and putting it in his pocket but the new Petey was driving the old Petey hard. And so the star glittered like a target.

The "'O Sole Mio Gaming House for Caballeros"—according to the paint-blistered sign—was the source of the whirring wheel.

Petey stopped Pat outside and got down. Pat looked at Petey and Petey looked at Pat.

He went across the veranda and into the saloon and found that the place was dark and almost deserted.

When his eyes became adjusted to the light, he walked along the bar, all the way along it, until he stood at the far end in such a position that he could duck if he had to.

But that was only the old Petey taking precautions as ever. The new Petey not only owned the place but the bartender's soul, the gambler's holdout, the church in the square, the entire pueblo, Arizona, the United States, the world, the solar system and the universe as well as any other universes which might have been floating unknown through the heavens.

Petey cocked his foot up on the bar, cocked his hat over one eye, cocked his head at the bartender and said, definitely, "Gimme a shot of carbolic acid and don't go dilutin' it none with strychnine!"

The bartender, being a Mexican, seeing the Ranger star, vacillated between diving out the back door and serving up the drink. Finally he conquered his wits by his commercial sense and served the drink.

Petey saw that the half a dozen men at the gaming table were staring at him. They were not very savory people, those men. They were in buckskin and leather and their eyes were like agates with St. Vitus. Their beards were black and white and gray, but all unshaven and untrimmed. Their hands, holding chips, had trigger fingers bent from long habit. They were, in short, the toughest fellows the old Petey had ever seen in his life. Undoubtedly one of them was Brad Thompson.

Petey sloshed the drink down his throat and the old Petey tried to cough and the new Petey growled, "Look here, greaser, I didn't come to this town to play pattycake with a bunch of sissies like them gents over at that table."

The men at the table stiffened. A sheepherder who had been asleep against the wall suddenly woke up, stared aghast at Petey and then slid like an eel out the door to immediately start running, despite the heat.

Petey's grin would have made a wolf die of heart failure.

"I come to this town," said Petey to the Mexican, "to generally work upon a gent named Brad Thompson, a penny-ante tinhorn and a coyote-hearted chicken thief. I come to this town alone because I likes action and if Petey McGuire came to town with company, there wouldn't be no action. You've heard of me?" he challenged.

The Mexican gulped, "Ah . . . ah . . ."

"Yeah, sure you have. Petey McGuire, the terror of the Mississippi, the scourge of Kansas and now the pride of the Arizona Rangers."

How the old Petey shivered at that invitation to death!

The new Petey insolently surveyed the room and pushed back his flat-brimmed hat and took off his right gauntlet and flexed his right hand. He took out his gun, pinwheeled it and tossed it up. He kicked out his hip and the six-gun slid into his holster.

"If Brad Thompson ain't scared to show himself," said Petey, "he's goin' back to Cristobal. Dead or alive, Petey McGuire don't care which!"

A shadow was in the doorway. The old Petey saw a

match-thin fellow in a frock coat standing there. The man's eyes were two live coals burning in the center of his head and his lips were pulled back to display long sharp teeth, dazzling white. The fellow was hung together so loosely that he looked like a rattlesnake wearing boots.

"Was somebody pagin' me?" said Brad Thompson hopefully.

Petey straightened up with an insolent grin. "Yeah. You'n me are going to take a trip and it's up to you, feller, whether you go tied across the saddle or sittin' straight up."

Brad Thompson took his choice with such suddenness that Petey barely had time to duck behind the bar before a bullet broke his glass into a flash of white light.

And Brad Thompson's smoke was so thick before him that he fired three times at the place where Petey had been.

Another gun spoke about a foot above the floor and Thompson did a dance step on the order of a pirouette to bring up hard against the wall. He tried to catch the gun as it fell from his right hand and the effort unbalanced him. He thudded prone upon the floor.

"Keep your seats, gentlemen," said Petey, stepping forth. "Your esteemed feller citizen don't need no company in the hospital."

The citizens kept their seats.

Petey walked over and hauled Brad to his feet. The man's shoulder was punctured and his head bruised from hitting the wall. Petey shook some life into him and then marched him out of the saloon.

Petey looked at Pat and winked and some dust got in Pat's eye and he winked back.

Chapter Four

CAPTAIN SHANNON sat at his desk. A shaded lamp at his elbow sent out a circle of yellow light which did not come up higher than Shannon's rocklike jaw. He had laid his watch on the scarred top and it tick-ticked loudly in tune to a locust which tick-ticked monotonously in the fragrant night. The hands were slowly clenching at midnight.

Shannon was not a nervous man. He could sit for hours without moving as though conserving his strength until he needed to uproot the Rocky Mountains.

His mind persisted in running over and over the same ground.

The kid was just a bluff. The kid had to be just a bluff. He had lighted out for California already and would never touch Cristobal again.

The kid had to be a bluff.

Shannon did not quite know why that was, would not let himself quite know. But the fact was there and as the watch and cricket ticked, so ticked the monotonous words: The kid had to be a bluff.

And then came a far-off sound which steadily grew into eight hoofs on the hard road. Eight hoofs as two mounts came at an even walk.

It must be Cole and Stevens, come back after their check on the bank job at Russell. Yes, that was it. It had to be Cole and Stevens.

In the compound the two mounts stopped and first one saddle creaked and then the other. Four feet sounded on the 'dobe pavement without the door and two spurs were merrily jingle bobbing and two heels were listless and shuffling.

The door was flung back.

Shannon lifted the shade of the lamp, blotting himself out and throwing the callers into full light.

The kid was standing there with a cocky swagger to his shoulders, with an insolent grin upon his lips. And the kid was holding up gray-faced and scared Brad Thompson.

"You needn't have sat up," said Petey to Shannon. "Hell, don't you think Petey McGuire can take care of these things by himself, huh? Come on, Thompson, don't get so shaky in the knees. I won't hurt you."

Thompson flicked his eyes from the kid to Shannon as a rattler flicks out his forked tongue. "Yeah, you got me now. Sure, you got me. But you can't do nothin' with me, neither of you. You can lock me up but you can't prove a damned thing on me!"

"Calm down," said Petey. "Well, Pop, do I have to put him away too?"

It was a challenge. Shannon knew it.

Three Rangers of the guard had crowded into the door behind Petey, their leathery faces taut with surprise as they looked at Thompson.

"Randolph," said Shannon, "lock Thompson up and get a doctor for him. I'll talk to him in the morning."

The three Rangers advanced and took Thompson who tried to push them off. They pulled him out of the office and were gone. Petey still stood there but now he advanced and sat on the edge of the desk. He gave the shade of the lamp a hard bat and it tilted up to glare into Shannon's eyes. Petey built himself a cigarette as he spoke.

"Pop, you thought you had me." He laughed amusedly to himself. "Yeah, you thought you had Petey McGuire, but you didn't know nothin'. It was a cinch. I invited the whole damned town to a war and this Thompson was the only one that'd drag his iron. And so I had to plug him on an even break. There wasn't no use to kill him so I took the soft muscle in his shoulder about a quarter of an inch above his collarbone and slammed him back against the wall and here he is."

Shannon said nothing.

Petey lit the cigarette by scraping a match over the desk top and then applying it. He threw the burned stick on the rug.

"Pop, you ain't any judge of men," said Petey. "I hear you was once the roughest, toughest, rootity-tootinest sky-hooter in Arizona." Petey laughed a little. "But you're slippin'. You're gettin' bald and blind. You got the place buffaloed, but they don't know the truth that you couldn't hit the broad side of a barn door. You're just about through, Shannon. You had me on a spot, you thought. Well, I come back. I come back and before this year is done . . . Yeah. Yeah, you expect to be made the head of all the Rangers. But you won't never be. I'm out for that job, Shannon. I'll get that job because compared to me you're about as lethal as a mesquite bush."

He got up, blew smoke through the gloom, and then jingle bobbed carelessly to the door. He slammed it behind him.

Shannon sat very still. He had not yet started to think.

And then he heard Bette's voice outside. Bette sounded like she wanted to cry. "You got back, Petey! I . . . I knew that Thompson would try to kill you. I knew it!"

Petey was most casual, Shannon noted bitterly. "Look here, sweetheart, don't go runnin' around in this night air without a jacket. Me, I'm tough and you're wastin' your time worryin' about me. Don't worry, just look and admire. Now get back to bed before something happens to you."

The voices faded away and Shannon sat still. At last he reached up and adjusted the lampshade and then he stared at the place Petey had sat. Shannon's cold gray eyes were growing hot.

"So you're out for my job," mouthed Shannon, never making a sound. "So I'm Pop and I'm old and you're going to get the chief Ranger's job before the year is done."

He saw a sudden vision of Bette, saw her in Petey McGuire's arms, looking worshipfully up at him. . . .

He saw Bette left and lost and alone and he saw himself done and dead and unable to help her.

He saw his own wife in her casket and suddenly, his own face, a young face with an insolent grin looking at a slip of a girl and telling her she'd belong to him someday. Yes, he'd won her. He'd won her and then to protect her he had become the toughest man in the Southwest.

And now Bette was going the same route but with a rotten guide. Petey McGuire could never love Bette. He was not worthy of Bette.

For twenty years Shannon had tried to shield that girl. He had had to be tough. He had had to guard her in this rugged country. He had protected her, gruffly, from the ruthless hands of lawless men and he would protect her now.

Petey McGuire was shallow and rotten, a man without a heart. He'd take what he wanted and throw the girl aside. And Shannon would not be there to help her.

He knew with a blinding flash of light that he was done, did Shannon. He was done as long as McGuire lived. For his whole life, Shannon had been fighting on the side of the law and the law had been behind him. And enemies there were. Too many enemies for the counting. And if, at last, those merciless, revengeful men knew that Shannon had been bested by an insolent kid, they would come and try their luck, afraid of the gunman reputation no longer.

Shannon jerked to his feet and stood staring at the door. Suddenly he paced around his desk and took a rifle down from its rack on the wall. But the steel was cold in his hands.

He slammed the rifle back.

He went back to his chair.

He looked at the flickering flame in the lamp and by it his glance was chill and calculating.

Yes. All he had to do was wait. Petey McGuire had gotten Thompson. But there were harder, more murderous jobs. Many jobs wherein it would be impossible for one man, alone, to do his work and come back alive.

Chapter Five

BRAD THOMPSON was not unintelligent. He had been a little of everything before he had seen great profit in selling other people's beef. He had originally come from New York where he had been kicked around the gutters until he reached the sour old age of twelve and then he had spent some time as the guest of Uncle Sam in a stone hotel. That had added to his bitterness as, despite the things he *had* done, he had not been guilty of the robbery of which he had been convicted.

Rolling westward, the practice of many years had made him lightning with a gun and able to ride a saddled thunderbolt without pulling leather.

But he had been too often double-crossed for him to have any faith in humanity. And so he was nervous and suspicious and more than once he had drawn and shot before any real menace had been visible in a man. His killings had mounted.

A year before, in Prescott, he had seen a Ranger walking serenely down the dusty street and the sudden thought had come to him that the Ranger was out to get him. And though the Ranger was really dwelling upon a drink and a girl, the Ranger died with a slug in his back.

And now Brad Thompson knew that he would soon see

how it felt to walk up thirteen steps and dangle his rattlesnake body from a noose while his spurs jingled from dancing lightly upon the air.

He knew he was done.

And that made him think hard and fast.

He let the wound heal under care for a week. It had stiffened his arm and always his arm would be stiff. But he let them pay the doctor bill and in the cell practiced a left draw without a gun. Nobody saw him. He was most docile. He joked with the Ranger sentry and all in all, made himself so pleasant that Bette one day sent him a slice of pie on the statement of his reputation.

She did things like that and then frightened herself with them afterwards because they seemed very bold and inviting.

And so it was. Brad saw her walking across the compound and gripped the window bars and watched her. She was all unknowing.

And that night Johnson, the Ranger sentry on duty at the moment, took Brad his supper.

Five hours later they found Johnson with his head crushed down into his face, sprawled in Brad's empty cell.

And Brad had vanished.

By half-troops, Rangers searched the country. Singly they scouted the towns. Grimly they watched and listened for news of Thompson.

They got it often enough. All of it was bad. He was still in the country but if he had been a desperate man before, he was a howling devil now. Rustling he abandoned and about him began to congregate certain gentlemen who saw profit and protection in sharing his fame.

And from May until mid-July, the reign of Brad Thompson went on in full swing and Shannon lost count of dead men found in burned ranches and strongboxes lost from the Overland Stage. And through the country echoed Thompson's repeated statement that he was hopefully waiting to kill a man named Petey McGuire.

The day had been hot and in contrast, the night was cold and all the brilliant stars were cupped above the earth to shed a soft and wonderful glow out of their crystal brilliance.

Shannon stepped out on the veranda before his office and looked across the dim compound. As he had expected, Petey McGuire was sitting on the barrack steps, all alone, looking at a lighted window in Shannon's house and dreaming dreams.

"McGuire!"

Petey stood up with a start. He had been a universe away. That was the old Petey and the new Petey had been asleep. But now the new Petey woke up with a snap and began to saunter idly down the walk toward the yellow rectangle upon which Shannon was silhouetted.

Shannon watched with narrowed disapproval, withdrawing as Petey approached so that when Petey entered, the Ranger captain was entrenched behind his desk.

Petey sat down in a rawhide chair, dangling one spurred boot as he indolently lighted a cigarette. "You had something to say to me?"

Shannon pushed his lamp back a couple feet and then looked squarely at Petey, finding it difficult to look McGuire in the eye.

"McGuire, there's a new governor coming out to take charge of the territory."

"Why tell me?" said Petey. "Think maybe I can talk him into making you chief of the Rangers?"

Shannon let the challenge pass. "He'll be coming by Overland Stage and he'll be here within the next two weeks. I want to have this section of country quieted down before he arrives."

"So he'll appoint you to the top post," said McGuire.

Shannon went on but he was not looking Petey in the eye at all. He was twisting a hunting knife around and around on his desk, an action most unusual for "nerveless" Shannon.

"McGuire, Brad Thompson is still on the loose. He's collected about fifteen men of the worst kind and rustling doesn't interest them as much as payrolls and gold."

Petey said not a word. He couldn't.

"And," said Shannon, "I had an idea that a tough man like yourself," and he edged it with sarcasm, "might succeed where half the troop might fail—where it has failed."

Still Petey could not push a word out of his tight throat.

"We know fairly definite that Thompson," continued Shannon, "is holding out in Buell Canyon but he can run away if too many try to attack the place." He couldn't look up at all now. "If one man were to attempt to arrest Thompson, he might succeed. And as you happen to be convinced that you are the toughest man in Cristobal . . ." Shannon took a deep breath which was almost a sob, "you can go get Brad Thompson again. . . . Alone."

Petey didn't say anything for minutes. Shannon did not look up.

Suddenly the old Petey knocked back the new Petey and spoke nervously. "Last time . . . last time it was different. Thompson was alone in Grande Piedras. But . . . but this time he's in the middle of a gang. One . . . one man couldn't walk in on him. He'd . . . he'd get *killed.*"

Shannon was silent for a long time and then he raised his head and gave Petey a stabbing glance. "You wouldn't be scared, would you, Mr. Petey McGuire?"

Petey sat still and his cigarette smoldered untouched.

Shannon pushed his advantage. "You wouldn't be showing the white feather, would you, Mr. Toughest Ranger?"

Petey put both feet on the floor. He felt sick at his stomach and Shannon's desk was leaping up and down and the room was whirling.

"Sure," said Shannon, "sure a man might get killed doing it, but Petey McGuire couldn't be scared of *anything.*" Shannon sat back, almost smiling. "All you do is walk into Buell Canyon and yank Thompson out of his crowd or kill Thompson in his crowd. Certainly fifteen gunslingers wouldn't stop Jehovah McGuire."

Petey's voice was hoarse. "He's been saying everywhere that he'd kill me on sight."

"Certainly," said Shannon, very cheerful now. "Certainly. And you've got your chance to call him a liar and show him that he can't kill you."

They didn't speak for more than five minutes. Petey sat hunched forward. He couldn't talk. The lamp laid a yellow pool of light upon the floor and he stared at the center of it.

In the quarters upstairs a light footstep sounded, repeated, and then was gone.

Suddenly Petey looked up and knew it had been Bette. Suddenly Petey got to his feet and the grin on his face was grisly in its contempt.

He walked forward and sat down on the edge of Shannon's desk and leaned forward, his Colt jutting away from his thigh and glittering in the lamplight. His eyes had aged a score of years.

"I understand now, Shannon. I understand. You're scared, that's all. Scared. You think I'll get your job. You think I'll steal your girl. You think I'm rotten all the way through but instead of coming out with it like a man you're using your job to kill me."

It was neither the old nor the new Petey speaking. It was a man whose throat was acrid as he tasted death.

Shannon looked at the top of his desk and then at Petey's Colt.

"You've been waiting for this," said Petey. "Sure. Sure. You think I can kill Thompson but you know I'll never get back alive."

Petey got up and gave his cartridge belt a hit. His gaze on Shannon was bleak as Shannon's own.

"And if I show the white feather," said Petey, "then you've also got me. You can . . ." He stopped. A footfall had sounded on the second floor again.

Petey put his fists down on Shannon's desk. "You know what's going to happen. But it won't. I'm going out to get Brad Thompson so you can make a show for the new governor. But I promise you, Shannon, I promise you that I'll come back. I'll get through and come back to Cristobal and take your girl and take your job." He stood up straight and hitched his belt again. "Yes," he added quietly. "Yes, I think I'll do that, Shannon."

Petey about-faced and walked to the door.

Shannon stared at the squared shoulders and suddenly Shannon wanted to yell at Petey to come back. But he didn't.

Chapter Six

FOR two weeks no word came to Cristobal about Ranger Pete McGuire.

And the tension grew.

For two weeks Captain Shannon listened with but half an ear to reports, reviewed with but half an eye and spoke with only half his thoughts.

From midnight until midnight he gave attention to the big arched gate and watched for a sorrel horse—or for a wide-swinging rider to come and say that a man was dead and that man was Petey McGuire.

For the first few days Shannon justified himself to the best of his ability. The boy was a braggart, on the owl-hoot trail. McGuire had nothing inside him but the glory of McGuire.

And to let such a man challenge his job, to let such a man crush the thing he held most dear . . . Shannon was not built that way.

But a thing happened.

Bette Shannon sat silently across the long dining table, white of face in contrast to the gay Mexican pottery, her gaze fixed upon the plate she had not touched.

The Mexican serving woman came silently on moccasined

feet and took the plate away and then, an instant later, hoofbeats sounded on the road outside the fort.

Bette was up and at the window, throwing back the drapery before Shannon knew that she had risen.

But it was only a mounted messenger from Prescott and from the way he rode he had no news of importance.

Bette came back to the table. A cup of coffee was there in a red cup and she warmed her hand about it as though that hand was cold.

Shannon eyed her thoughtfully.

Suddenly she lifted her gray eyes to his and he was startled at the brilliance of them, at the strength behind them.

"Are you keeping any news from me?"

Shannon shook his head. "No. Nothing's happened that I know about. Cole and Stevens . . ."

"Damn Cole and Stevens!" said this girl who had looked so frail. "You know what I mean. Where is Petey McGuire?"

Shannon stared at her and didn't like what he saw. He had never thought she could get angry.

She stood up, trembling, but not from anything but the violence of storm within her. Her head was proud and her small mouth courageously set.

"Are you holding back what you know?" she demanded.

"Now," said Shannon placatingly, "don't get so upset, Bette. He is merely doing his duty, accepting the challenge of Thompson and"—he could not stay the shaft—"if McGuire is as good as he says he is, all is going well."

"You're lying!" said Bette. "I know what you did and I know

why you did it! You ordered him out, *alone.* You ordered him out on a job when you should have sent your entire troop! You sent him to die because you hate him, because you're afraid of him!"

He tried to stop her. He had never known that such depths of emotion lay within this girl. She had always been so obedient to him, always so anxious to please him. . . .

"Bette, please . . ."

"I've been afraid of you all my life!" said Bette. "I've tried to reach you and you've held me off. I've been ordered around like a trooper. I couldn't talk to people you didn't want me to talk to. I had to wear the dresses you liked. . . . Yes, I've been afraid of you. And why not! You're a granite mountain without any heart. You're a killer so cold that you would send a kid out to die just because you were afraid of what that boy might do. Oh, yes, you did!"

"Duty . . ." began Shannon, but he got no farther.

Her scorn was like the flashing lightning. "Duty! What do you know of duty! You're Shannon. Shannon the killer! Ranger or outlaw, it makes no difference. You're proud of your record and when a slim boy comes with courage enough to challenge you, then you won't give him the even break about which you prate! Oh, no! You use your authority to send him out to die!"

"Bette!" said Shannon sharply.

"Bette!" she mocked him. "What am I? A trooper? Bette! Yes, squads right and wheel left and right front into line! That's all you know. But I'm no trooper, I'm a woman and I can't be broken. Oh, you almost did break me. Yes, almost. And then a kid named Petey McGuire came and gave me back my soul."

He stood up so suddenly that he knocked over his chair. "Go to your room!"

"You haven't nerve enough to touch me," said Bette, head up and shoulders squared. "You can't touch me because you know I'm right!"

Shannon mastered himself. "He volunteered. . . ."

"And so you can lie about it!" cried Bette.

"You accuse . . ."

"Never mind what I accuse because I know. I know, Captain Shannon. At midnight, too many days ago to remember, Petey McGuire was saddling his horse at the stables. I heard you downstairs. Yes, I listened to you and heard everything that was said. And I went to the stables and found Petey. Braggart, is he? Heartless, is he? No courage, has he? Those things are lies.

"Petey went after Thompson, and he's still after him or dead, Captain Shannon, but Petey McGuire left this fort after . . ."

"Bette!"

"And he told me! He told me what he was and why he was. And after he had told me, he was gone.

"And, Captain Shannon, if Petey McGuire does not come back alive, all Arizona is going to know that the iron-hard Shannon is a yellow dog at heart!"

She turned and walked to her room and long after the door

had slammed, Shannon stared at it. He stared at it bleakly. McGuire had won. Yes, dead or not, McGuire had won.

And everything for which Shannon had thought he stood had become a crumbled ruin. His reputation, his girl, his life.

They were in the hands of a kid named Petey McGuire, a kid that had cried against the breast of a girl.

Chapter Seven

IT was hot beside the two wheel tracks which made the road. It was hot and up on high, a buzzard, scenting death, wheeled and wheeled on muted wings to watch the lone rifleman who lay between two boulders.

The sun had baked through Petey's vest, through his shirt, through his back, and down to his star. He felt like a spitted fowl. The gun barrel was so hot to his touch that he had put on his gauntlets so that he could hold it.

Down in a canyon Pat was grazing, out of sight but stopping every few minutes to raise his head and focus his ears and wonder why his master had told him he had to stay there, wondering if everything was all right on the other side of the rim. The grass was luscious but Pat was not taking much interest in it. Petey had been nervous and quick.

And Petey was still nervous and quick.

He had waited four hours.

The Overland had been robbed four days before. It had been robbed two weeks before. It had been robbed a month before. And each time it had happened in the most likely spot west of the last spot.

And it would be here if anywhere that the overdue stage would be halted by Brad Thompson.

On the stage would be an extra guard. But messengers had

their own ideas about the value of their lives despite the pep talks given them by Wells Fargo agents.

The road was thirty feet below Petey. No one could see him except from above and only that expectantly hungry buzzard was in the blue.

Through the gray boulders wandered the wagon tracks. Past two huge boulders which could easily hide half a hundred men.

It was an ideal spot.

And Brad Thompson had already picked it out. The tracks of his riders on inspection of the place had been clear to Petey. Men had ridden to this place, dismounted for a surveyal and had then picked posts. They had mounted again to ride on.

The whole story was down there in the sand.

And it was noon and the sun was unbearable and the place was so still that the silence rang monotonously.

The sound of hoofs came gradually down the trail. Petey stayed down, listening. He heard the cavalcade arrive and then Brad Thompson's voice issuing crisp and nervous orders. Dismounted men began to scatter.

Bootbeats were coming up the slope toward Petey's place. It was too ideal to be overlooked.

But he did not raise his head. He had time.

The man was scrambling and panting as he slipped in the shale. He had expected nothing between these two high rocks, he was too out of breath to shout.

Petey grabbed him by the neck and yanked him close. Petey's fist connected perfectly with the fellow's jaw. It was an angle punch. The man sighed and relaxed.

Petey hauled him back into the cleft and tied him up.

It was one of the men he had seen in Grande Piedras.

Petey took his position again. Nobody below had thought to watch one of the number take a position as everyone had been too busy finding his own.

Petey lay still and the sun again was hot. Time dragged. Dust settled and nothing could be seen along the wagon road.

The sun gradually slanted down the sky. One o'clock. Two o'clock. Three o'clock . . .

Petey was exhausted. The man had come to and was muttering blackly into his gag.

Petey was coming close to the point where he would do anything to break the tension.

But wagon wheels broke it. Six horses in harness and wagon wheels.

On the run the stage was rocketing along this torturous trail. The Overland Stage was behind time and the driver's whip sizzled and cracked to the right and left of the leaders.

Petey did not raise up.

His ears told him that the stage was almost under him.

There came a scream of brakes and a volley of words in anger.

Then, "Joe! Get down and push them goddamn logs off the trail. Hurry it up. This might be . . ."

Brad Thompson's voice was harsh and commanding.

"Lift your paws, gents. Grab sky and shut up!"

There was a startled and concerted snort and the wagon creaked as the horses bunched.

Petey very carefully raised himself, hatless, to look down.

The stage was being flanked by men. Brad Thompson was stepping down from the boulders. His men were closing watchfully in, red bandanas with eye-slits in them covering all faces.

The driver had his hands high. The two messengers had dropped their rifles to the top of the coach and were also grabbing sky as ordered.

"Out of there, you," said Thompson.

From within came protest and anger. And then the door hinges creaked and out stepped a little butterball of a man in a gray suit and high-heeled boots. Behind him came a thin fellow and yet another sober-faced and thoroughly frightened gentleman.

The three passengers lined up beside the stage, reaching high.

Thompson stepped briskly to the hub of the right front wheel. "Throw down the express box!"

The driver very urgently jostled a messenger. And the messenger reached slowly and carefully down to start tipping the box over the edge.

Suddenly some madness gripped that messenger. He grabbed for his Henry rifle.

But he never touched its steel.

Brad Thompson fired at the range of ten feet and half the messenger's face vanished as he lunged sideways off the box.

Petey thrust his rifle ahead and his voice was strong. "Drop your guns!"

Thompson whirled, the others whirled.

The driver had his hands high. The two messengers had dropped their rifles to the top of the coach and were also grabbing sky as ordered.

Brad Thompson saw Petey McGuire up above between the boulders. The glimpse was enough. Thompson snapped a slug at the challenging voice and Petey's whole right arm went numb.

But he pulled the trigger.

The smoke was lazy as it followed the bullet.

And Brad Thompson seemed suddenly languorous. His Colt pinwheeled on his thumb and dropped. His knees buckled and he gripped at the wheel with a hand which knew it was dead.

Petey levered his Winchester. In the next ten seconds the air over his head was thick with the whistle and whine of lead and thunder rolled through the gorges.

Winchester empty, Petey began to lay on with his Colt.

And men dropped down there in the road. And other men scrambled for cover.

And when the first man began to run, messenger and driver, whipped to fury by the murder of their friend, gripped Henrys and began to pump lead.

And the little butterball of a man laid about him with a blunt .41.

Thunder rolled in the gorges. And then it echoed back to find the place of ambush still.

A horse was running far off on the plain. A nervous outlaw was holding up his hands to show they were empty. A small group of three were sprinting far off down the road, diving in and out of cover like quail.

And like quail, the three were shot as the last edge of rage depressed the triggers of the men on the coach.

It was still again.

The little butterball of a man was staring up at the cleft with wondering eyes. And then the rest began to look up.

Petey got to his feet and though his checkered shirt was stained, there was a cocky swagger in the way he stood looking down at the men of the Overland Stage.

He turned and rolled out the tied outlaw and sent him bumping down the short slope.

And then Petey followed, walking free, rifle in his left hand and revolver reloaded in its holster.

As he came to the side of the stage, he pulled his chin thong into place and tipped his hat back. His face was grimy with powder stains which made his smile startlingly white and frank.

He turned Brad Thompson over with his foot and the man's arms flopped out and the eyes stared at the buzzard which still wheeled overhead—stared without seeing bird or sky.

Petey McGuire whistled shrilly. He did not seem to know he was hurt. In a few seconds hoofbeats were heard coming out of the canyon and then Pat swung into sight at a trot, empty stirrups flapping against his flanks.

Petey gave Pat a grin and a love-tap on the nose and then moved back to slide the Winchester into its boot.

Not until then did he seem to be aware of the astonished stares which were focused upon him. He surveyed them carelessly.

"Well, what are you waiting for?" said Petey. "Pick up the box and get going. You're hours late."

The little butterball of a man in the gray suit looked strangely at Petey McGuire and moved forward, extending his hand. Petey took it indifferently with his left.

"Son," said the little man, "I see that you are a Ranger by the star. But I'd like to know your name."

"Me? Me?" said Petey. "Why, I'm Petey McGuire, the toughest Ranger in Arizona."

Shocked a little by such immodesty, the little man caught sight of the sprawled Brad Thompson's corpse. And then the little man in gray smiled slightly.

"Yes?" he said.

"Yeah," said Petey. "That gent was out to get me and a certain captain . . . But to hell with that. Ask anybody in Arizona, they'll tell you who is Petey McGuire. And they'll tell you that I'll be chief of the Rangers before the year is out."

"So?" said the little man.

"Yeah," said Petey.

"You think you're old enough . . . ?"

"Me? Age don't have a thing to do with it. I'm Petey McGuire and I'm tough. And now, if you want to get to Grande . . ."

"Wait," said the little man. "Are you really going to be the chief of Rangers?"

"Yeah," said Petey.

"Then," said the little man, "if you say you are, I am no man to mess into Fate. Let me be the first to congratulate you."

"Huh?" said Petey.

"Yes, you see I am Ralph Osborn, the new governor of the Territory of Arizona."

Chapter Eight

ALTHOUGH Petey's arm was in a sling and although he might have swaggered as he dismounted from Pat in the compound at Cristobal, he did not.

He walked with confidence, yes. But not with swagger. He exuded confidence, yes, but not cockiness.

There was something very real and certain about every move he made. Something frank about the way he smiled.

The old Petey and the new Petey had met at last on common ground.

And so Pete McGuire moved up the steps to Shannon's office as naturally as a confident man ever moved.

Shannon was waiting. He had known for two hours that McGuire was on his way.

And in those two hours, Shannon had gone through hell.

He was tired, was Shannon, tired and old. And death was close at hand. As soon as men knew . . .

Pete McGuire came up to the desk and sat down on its corner.

He was aware of a girl in white standing in the door. But he did not dare turn. Not yet. He did not dare let them know that he knew. He had something to say.

"Shannon," said McGuire, "you're through."

Shannon looked up at the youngster. There was nothing

granite about Shannon now. He was just an old man sitting in a creaky chair.

"You wanted," said McGuire, "the post of chief Ranger. You've lost it because I'm that man. Yes, you probably heard about it already because I had to get patched up."

"Please," said Shannon feebly. "Please, McGuire. I was out of my head. I didn't know what I was doing. I tell you freely that you were right. I was trying to put you out. . . ."

"Shut up," said Petey. "I don't want to hear about it because I know about it. But I can't blame you much. Reputation, daughter, job . . . Yes, you saw them going."

Shannon was whipped and knew it. He was quiet.

"But you're through here too," said Petey. "You're no longer a Ranger captain."

"I got it coming," whispered Shannon.

"No," said Petey, standing up with an expansive grin, "you'll never be the chief of the Rangers and you're through here at this job because . . ."

"Please," begged Shannon.

But an astounding thing had happened. Petey had stretched forth his left hand and Shannon, not understanding, took it hesitantly.

"Because," said Petey with an even wider grin, "we are sending you as the next senator from Arizona to the United States capital at Washington. And, Pop, let me be the first to congratulate you."

Petey didn't want to see tears in a hard man's eyes. So he turned and walked toward Bette who waited for him there by the door.

The Ranch That No One Would Buy

The Ranch That No One Would Buy

HE had the stillest blue eyes God ever put into a man. They were the first things anyone noticed about him. But further inspection revealed that the rest of him had the same quality as his eyes.

He was quiet. His spurs didn't jingle, his belt didn't creak. Mounting or dismounting there was never a sound from his saddle. His horse followed his master's example and nobody ever remembered hearing the little black pony so much as whicker.

He came into Faro with the heat of the day, never making a sound. His eyes were on his back trail before he entered the town; very quietly on his back trail as though he was afraid that a breath from him would call down upon him all the demons from Hell.

He walked the black pony silently down the dusty street, sitting his saddle as though he expected a bullet in his back. He looked at the signs of the shabby cow town, reading them one by one and still watching the few men in sight—and from his look, he would have showed no surprise if every one of them had whirled about to begin shooting at him.

He carefully surveyed the Silver Dollar Saloon and Hotel, and though he seemed to give no directions, the little black pony put his decision into action and approached the hitchrack there.

There were idlers on the porch with their ever-curious stares. They made him uneasy. He did not do more than drop the reins; the black pony understood.

For everyone else the steps of the Silver Dollar creaked. But not for him.

For everyone else the porch groaned under the slightest weight. But not his.

For everyone else the swinging doors sang a dismal dirge. But they were still as he pushed through them.

The clerk looked up with a start. He had heard nobody approach and long residence in the Silver Dollar had frayed his wearied nerves. But he was instantly at ease. There could be no menace in so still a man.

The clerk laid down his pen and rubbed his bald head, leaving a bluish streak of ink there to match the real veins. He eyed his prospective guest, adding him up as well as he could.

This man was young. And though he might have been a puncher, his face was not windburned. The texture of his skin was delicate, almost like a girl's. And his hands on the desk were long-fingered and white. He was not from this part of Texas. Nor were his tailored shirt and chaps Californio.

The clerk was puzzled. "Y'come far, stranger?"

"Far enough," said the other in a smooth, quiet voice which bore more than a hint of a drawl. He smiled uncertainly. "Have you a room, suh?"

"Number five. Cash in advance, sign here," parroted the clerk. And when the other had signed he slewed the ledger around and devoured the neat signature. "Jerry Delaney, huh? Y'didn' fill in no town."

"Make it . . . make it Pecos," said Delaney.

"Oh, I read your brand now," said the clerk. "Shore. Old Bab Thompson writ me about you. It'd have to be a stranger that'd buy his spread. The local capital has got better sense."

Two shabby men across the lobby grew conspicuously quiet at the mention of the names.

"Y'goin' out today?" persisted the clerk.

"After Stardust has a rest. What . . . what is the matter with the ranch, suh?"

"Stardust. Now ain't that a purty name fer a hoss."

"Is something wrong with the Rocking T?" said Delaney, his anxiety almost hidden by his slow drawl.

"Y'goin' to be around fer a couple hours?" said the clerk. "I'll tell the county clerk yer in town and y'kin fix up yer papers. How come you thunk up a hoss name like that?" All the while he spoke he stared at the men across the room, still conspicuously quiet.

Delaney turned and looked at the pair. Uneasily he hitched his saddlebags up on his arm. His hand was shaking a trifle. "Number five, you say? I'll go up, if you don't mind, suh, and then walk around and see to Stardust."

"Make yerself to home," said the clerk.

Delaney walked up the rickety steps and put his saddlebags in the room. He came down—the steps did not creak—and passed the clerk. He stopped for an instant when he saw that the lobby loungers had left. He shivered slightly and then went on out.

The clerk had watched him leave with mixed emotions. It seemed a shame for such a good-looking young fellow to walk into a mess like the Rocking T. And at the same time, Lush Wilson, the clerk, had very little respect for a man that showed his lack of nerve.

He had not much time to ruminate. Smoke Lassiter banged through the swinging doors, bootbeats loud and face clouded. He swung to the bar and stamped his foot down on the rail. He knocked a glass to the floor by way of calling Lush Wilson's attention. Like trained hounds upon their master's heels, the two shabby individuals sidled up behind Lassiter.

Lush Wilson made haste. Smoke's red-rimmed eyes, small for his big face, were danger signals. Lush set out the bottle.

"So he got here!" said Lassiter, immediately throwing off a drink. "What kind of a lookin' gent is he?"

"He's—" began one of the men.

"Shut up," snapped Lassiter.

"He's just a kid," said Lush Wilson. "There ain't no percentage in killin' kids, Smoke."

Lassiter's hand dived for his gun butt and stayed there, tense. "Why, you blabber-mouthed coyote! Who the hell are you callin' a killer?"

"Nobody," said Lush in a small voice. "But he ain't no gunman. He's just a kid. He . . . he calls his hoss Stardust and his hands aren't like yours and mine. They're—"

"Stardust!" exploded Lassiter with a guffaw. "So that's the kind of gent that bought the Rocking T. This is easy! If Bab Thompson didn't have the guts to stay and face me, this kid'll run a mile on sight of me! Set 'em up, Lush. It's on your house."

Lush set 'em up obediently. "I dunno why," he said cautiously, "you don't just buy the Rocking T—"

"Who's got seventy thousand dollars in these times?" snapped Lassiter. "Since that damned Land Office crowd made such a smell, a guy's got to be careful. First thing you know—"

"It'll be a hangin' offense to kill a man," finished Lush. "It's your game, Smoke, not mine. But it seems a kind of a shame. He's such a purty kid."

"Aw, I won't kill him," said Smoke. "Not unless he gets stubborn. What good would he be to me dead? He's got to have enough life in him to sign papers, ain't he? And I'll make it legal too. I'll pay him the seventy thousand after—"

"Look, Smoke," said Lush Wilson, "I know what you can do and I'm in this thing as deep as you are because of the cash I advanced. But I'm askin' you not to kill this kid. Leave him alone. I'll take my loss—"

"You go chicken-hearted on me, Wilson," said Lassiter, "and the wolves'll be havin' a good time with your corpse. This country is gettin' civilized. Another few years and we won't have pickin's like these. C'mon, Eddie, we'll look over his baggage. Keep your eye peeled, Slewfoot, in case the marshal looks in. What he don't know won't hurt him."

Smoke, with Eddie at his heels, went thunderously up the

creaking steps. He strode into number five and picked up the saddlebags. With fingers which were clumsy everywhere except around a gun, he undid the silver buckles.

A letter came to light and Smoke moved to the fly-specked window to read it.

> Gerald Delaney
> New Orleans
>
> Dear Son:
>
> I am only too glad to have this chance to help you. The enclosed draft for sixty-five thousand dollars gives you a little leeway in your deal. When you get everything set, I'll come down and see you. Sorry about your bad luck in New Orleans.
>
> My very best, Mother

"Huh," said Smoke. "Postmarked St. Louis. Old Bab must've come down in his price after he lit out."

He moved back to the saddlebags and replaced the letter. For several minutes he rummaged through the neatly packed clean clothes. At last a card in the very bottom came to his attention.

He stared at it and then gave a booming laugh. Thunder in his throat, he clattered down into the lobby and confronted Lush Wilson.

"No wonder that kid's scared stiff!" chortled Smoke.

Wilson looked at the card and blinked. "No wonder," he whistled.

Eddie and Slewfoot peered at it and giggled in chorus.

"He had plenty of reason for runnin' away from New

Orleans," said Wilson. "Better men than him haven't stayed to face that music. I thought he looked nervous when he came in and didn't think Bab had explained this deal to him."

"Look how he's thumbed it," said Smoke. "I bet he's put in plenty of time and put out plenty of sweat studyin' this thing."

He read it aloud, "'Jacques Duval.'" He turned it over and read the handwriting on the back: "'You will do me the pleasure of meeting me tomorrow at dawn ashore from Bayou Margarite. I shall furnish both pistols and coffee. Should you lack funeral funds, my lawyer will arrange everything.'"

The two shabby individuals were both very amused because Smoke was amused. But now their curiosity got the better of them. "Who is Jacques Duval?" said Eddie.

Smoke turned a withering stare of scorn upon him. "If you'd keep your nose out of a whiskey glass, you might know something. Jacques Duval is the greatest duelist in New Orleans. Look at him wrong and he sends a challenge and kills his man. 'Who is Jacques Duval?'" he mimicked in disgust.

"You know him?" said Eddie, popeyed.

"*Know* him?" said Smoke. "After all the time I put in, in New Orleans? I was the only guy he wouldn't challenge."

"What's he look like?"

"Tall, sallow-faced guy. Must be about forty now. Hasn't got an ounce of mercy in him. Hell with the ladies. Sleeps with a pistol in one hand and a rapier in the other. Husbands down in New Orleans always knock when they come home late. That's Jacques Duval for you. No wonder this kid was running away!"

The doors groaned as they swung inward and the men at the bar whipped about to identify the newcomer. He was a stoutish man in gray tweeds, but for all his squat bulk there was a furtiveness in his flushed face. His personality was a cross between an ox and a rabbit.

Smoke grinned. "Howdy, Consadine."

"Hello, Smoke," said Consadine, glancing about the lobby as though expecting to turn up a rattlesnake.

"The buzzards assemble," muttered Lush Wilson.

"I heard the new owner of the Rocking T was in town," said Consadine carelessly.

Smoke chuckled. "Yeah. You wouldn't be getting any fancy ideas, would you, Consadine? A deal's a deal, unless you want to get buried."

Consadine quaked. "Oh, I didn't mean nothin', Smoke. I'm willin' to play the game. IXL is gettin' some impatient, but what they don't know can't hurt them, and as long as I'm agentin' for them—"

"You'll cut all the throats in sight," finished Smoke with an ugly snort. "I'll bet they're payin' you a hundred and fifty thousand."

"A hundred and twenty, I swear it," said Consadine. "We'll clean up the fifty thousand clear after we pay the new owner seventy. But how you going to get him to sell?"

"That's easy," said Smoke. "He's a lily-livered kid. And the more I think of it—"

"The more you drink," amended Lush.

"The more I think of it," persisted Smoke, "the less reason I see for handin' seventy thousand over to the little yahoo."

"You aren't goin' to kill him?" said Consadine with a start.

"Naw," said Smoke, "but if he gets stubborn, he'll wish he was dead. Might see the deal through by tomorrow."

"Maybe he'll light out like Bab Thompson did," said Consadine.

"Yeah? A man can't light out without a hoss, can he?"

"You mean you'll steal his bronc?" said Consadine. "Hell, Smoke, that's goin' too far. They don't like hoss stealin' around here."

"Who's a thief?" challenged Smoke, hand darting to his gun.

Consadine blanched. "I didn't mean nothin'," he said weakly.

Smoke relaxed. "You can fix a hoss so he can't run."

"Not me," begged Consadine.

"Eddie here's an expert," stated Smoke. "Naw, our little friend ain't leavin' town until we got what we want." He took another drink. "And the more I think about it, the less reason I see for him to leave town at all. Maybe he'd squawk to the Land Office or the federal marshal or somebody. Yeah, maybe I think that would be a good idea."

"Not murder," pleaded Consadine.

"'Not murder,'" mimicked Smoke. "We're all in this together. What's a corpse more or less between friends?"

Consadine drifted toward the door. Nobody noticed his going and he went gently for fear they would. When he got out in the street he quickened his stride, approaching the livery stable.

When he reached the door he stopped. Only the newcomer was inside, though there were several horses in the place—among them Smoke Lassiter's buckskin.

When his eyes became accustomed to the dimness, Consadine could see the stranger more clearly. It startled him to find a man so young, so seemingly untouched by wind and sun.

He was about to approach and speak when the Rocking T's new owner spoke instead. But not to Consadine.

Delaney was sitting on the top of the stall division, looking at Stardust who contentedly munched his oats.

"You haven't so much farther to go," said Delaney in his quiet drawl. "It's all going to be different now. Did I ever tell you that one about the longest road?"

> There's peace in every sunset,
> Be it scarlet, gray or gold. . . .

"Poetry!" whispered the shocked Consadine to himself. "Sayin' poetry to a hoss!" It unnerved him.

"Hey!" said Consadine.

Delaney turned without a sound and looked at Consadine.

"I come out to see you," said Consadine. "Listen, you don't want the Rocking T, kid. I tell you what I'll do. I'll give you fifty thousand dollars for the spread—in case you'll sign the papers in the next half-hour, givin' us both time to leave town."

"Fifty thousand dollars?" drawled Delaney softly. "Mister, I paid sixty thousand for it and Mr. Thompson convinced me that it's worth a hundred and fifty."

"Did he tell you why he left town?"

"Why . . . no. He said something about his health being better in New Orleans."

"Huh! I'll say it is. Bab Thompson don't dare show his face around here on account of Smoke Lassiter."

"Who?"

"Smoke Lassiter. He's bad. He's killed a dozen men. If you'll sign up quick, I'll draw the cash from the bank and we can burn trail before he gets wise."

"I don't understand," said Delaney.

"You'll understand all right. He'll make you sell. Why the hell do you think Bab Thompson sold the Rocking T at such a loss? Where there's a bargain like that, there's usually a rattlesnake in the package. Come on, kid, get smart and unload."

"I see," said Delaney, suddenly sad. "I thought— Look, mister, I can't drop ten thousand dollars like that. I *can't.*"

"You better drop ten thousand before you drop sixty and your life in the bargain."

Delaney sat very still. At last he said, "You don't understand."

There was misery in his voice and Consadine was touched. There was something so graceful, even pretty, about this kid. "Look, it ain't too bad. I tell you what I'll do. I'll make it your sixty thousand back again. You can light out with clean hands."

The kid thought about it for a long time while Consadine nervously watched the door.

"No," said Delaney softly. "It isn't right. I told her I'd see it through this time. I'm not going to run away again."

"Again?" said Consadine.

"You don't understand," said Delaney. "I left New Orleans . . . because I . . . Forget it. No, I've got to see this through, mister. Besides, there isn't anybody going to kill me. Why should they want to?"

"I give up," said Consadine. "But I'll give you this warning: Don't go out to the Rocking T tonight. Stay in town until you know what you face."

He went away and left Delaney in a very thoughtful mood.

After a long time Delaney slid off the stall boards and gently pulled his pony's nose out of the oats. Stardust—so named because of the silver flecks on his forehead—looked wonderingly at his master. And he was presently more puzzled than ever.

Delaney walked silently out of the stable. He did not want to go back to the hotel. Slowly he strolled out from the town, wandering along the lanes of sage. A rattlesnake whirred somewhere at hand and he started. Carefully he walked far around it.

The heat of the day was growing less and the sun was sinking to turn the town and plain, dun by day, into a glowing canvas of pleasant colors. Delaney climbed a knoll and looked gratefully into the west, the wind gentle and cool against his face.

He sat down, drinking in the splendor, soothed by the immensity of the endless plain beneath the vast, inverted paint pot of the sky.

Unthinkingly he snipped a wildflower and ran the stem through his shirt button.

It was a long way back. He hadn't realized he had come so far and it was very black before he reached the town.

He found a place in a restaurant and sat with his back to the wall, eyeing the door as he ate. When he had finished, he drifted back to the Silver Dollar, which had come to life with the death of the sun.

Eddie slipped out of the restaurant behind him and hastened to the 'dobe hut where Smoke Lassiter lived. He emerged a moment later with the gunman.

Smoke buckled on his belts and tied down his guns. "You say he had a flower in his shirt?"

"Yeah," grinned Eddie.

Smoke laughed.

"His manners was enough to kill you off," said Eddie. "Dainty as a gal."

Smoke laughed again as Eddie pantomimed Delaney's actions.

They strode toward the Silver Dollar. Outside Smoke stopped. "You spotted his hoss this afternoon?"

"Yeah."

"Here's a knife."

"Okay."

Eddie drifted into the yellow-patched street.

Smoke looked after him for a moment and then went into the Silver Dollar.

The tables which had been covered against the dust that afternoon were now full and the kerosene lamps threw down their light into piles of chips and silver. The place was a beehive of hope and despair.

One table was empty of gamblers and the kid had seated

himself there to play a lonely game of solitaire. His fingers were clumsy with the cards.

Smoke glanced around the saloon and saw the town marshal. He frowned for a moment and then grunted under the impact of an idea.

He sidled up to Delaney. "Hello, youngster."

Delaney glanced up and said nothing.

"I'm Smoke Lassiter. I'm sort of a welcoming committee of one around Faro and I shore hates to see a guy sittin' by his lonesome playin' solitaire. That's a sheepherder's game."

Delaney still said nothing.

Smoke eased into the opposite chair and Slewfoot appeared from nowhere to take another.

"Would you mind a game of stud?" said Smoke.

Delaney hesitated, but there was something very compelling about Lassiter. Delaney swallowed hard. "I . . . I wouldn't mind."

Smoke relaxed. He called for a new deck and Lush Wilson hobbled across the room with it. Lush looked at Delaney. He seemed about to say something but thought better of it when he caught Smoke's abruptly dangerous eye.

Smoke broke the seal and began to shuffle. "We play a pretty steep game here. Blue's a quarter."

"I . . . I guess that's all right," said Delaney producing a double eagle.

Smoke expanded even more. He dealt with the quick practice of a gambler—and it was strange in view of his thick-fingered hands. One by one the cards slapped down.

The pot was about ten dollars when the kid turned up three jacks to beat Lassiter's two queens. Slewfoot folded his hand quietly.

Delaney appeared to take heart as he stacked the pot before him. Smoke grinned and winked covertly at Lush Wilson. Wilson walked away, disgusted.

The next deal was Delaney's. He was slow but precise and the cards made no sound whatever as he passed them around.

The pot got up to eight dollars. Delaney had a pair showing. So did Smoke, but Smoke hastily folded up and Slewfoot, starting to get interested—and having a visible straight—gave a grunt of pain and looked at Smoke with grieved eyes. Slewfoot folded up.

"Looks like your lucky night," said Smoke.

"Yes," said Delaney. "I'm pretty lucky at cards."

"That so?" said Smoke.

"Yes. I won a hundred dollars one night," said Delaney, expanding a little.

"A hundred dollars!" gaped Smoke. "Think of that! I bet your friends were sore."

"They didn't like it very much," said the kid, more expansive than ever.

Lush had come back and Smoke gave him a grin.

For the next hour the dollars persisted in stacking up before Delaney. And the more he won, naturally, the more he wanted to bet. He had two hundred and eight dollars and the sight of it before him was heady.

"Let's up the limit?" said Delaney.

Smoke scowled. "With your luck?"

"Well . . . you might have a chance to get it back."

"All right," said Smoke. "Lush, lend me five hundred, will you? I've got to get that two hundred back."

Lush produced the money from his safe.

The game went smoothly on and soon the five hundred in addition to the two hundred and eight were piled brightly before Delaney. Slewfoot had long dropped out. The game was beginning to attract attention. Smoke was looking dark. He made his bets savagely. He called for another five hundred.

Midway through his last stack of blues, Smoke looked sullenly at the kid's possible flush. He himself had a visible pair of aces. It took him a long time to make his decision. Finally he folded up.

The gallery looked surprised. Smoke wasn't showing much courage in this game. In fact he was playing very horrible stud.

But Delaney's eyes were shining and, though he said not a word, the pile before him made him radiate confidence.

The limit was upped again.

Hour after hour it went on. Again and again Smoke drew heavily on Lush Wilson and finally resorted to counter-signed IOUs which Delaney was only too glad to accept.

The gallery was now four deep. Five-hundred-dollar pots were beginning to be more and more frequent. Delaney looked drunk, though he had not touched a drop—refusing it politely. The dollars made him reckless.

It was near morning when the kid counted up his IOUs

before him, stopping the game for a moment. "Why . . . why, there's thirty thousand dollars here!"

"I'm good for it," snapped Smoke. "I've got a spread worth twice that."

The gallery was still.

Lush looked uncomfortable under Smoke's compelling glare. "Yeah," said Lush, "he's good for 'em. I back him up. I signed, didn't I?"

"Oh, I wasn't questioning anyone," said Delaney with haste.

"Play cards," growled Smoke, his eyes red-rimmed. "Gimme a drink, Lush."

It was Smoke's deal. With the final card, there was a thousand-dollar pot. The kid had a pair of jacks showing. Smoke had a possible straight. But Smoke had been plunging for a long, long time. The kid was used to his empty bluffs.

"Make it a thousand," said Smoke. "I'll draw short."

"A thousand, and another thousand," responded Delaney.

"Here's yours and I'm drawing mine."

"Call," said Delaney, thrusting out an IOU.

Smoke had his filler.

That was the first big pot Delaney had lost. It did not bother him.

Nothing bothered him the next many hands until he suddenly realized that he was out of IOUs and back to twelve hundred in cash. He looked quietly at that shrunken stack. But he was not bothered too much even then. And he had heard of a thing called sportsmanship. He had to give Smoke his chance.

The twelve hundred vanished. But Delaney's fever had not.

It was growing late—or rather, very early. Big bets had become such a habit that the kid lost five thousand on the next pot until . . .

Smoke was sure of his game now. In a moment he would get the Rocking T in a perfectly legal way. He had built his structure nicely.

But when he reached out to take that five-thousand-dollar pot on the strength of three aces, one buried after his deal, Delaney made a motion to stop him.

"Just a minute," said the kid wonderingly. "You've got the ace of spades against my three kings showing."

"What's wrong with that?" challenged Smoke.

Quietly the kid turned over his own hole card. It was the ace of spades.

Smoke was quick. He lunged to his feet. "Why, you dirty little rat! Trying to welch on that pot by sliding in a card! The last man that called me cheat was planted!"

The crowd swept back from behind Delaney.

Smoke, driven to save his face, was a towering fury. Deliberately he smashed Delaney across the mouth.

The kid went backwards out of his chair. He did not get up. Holding a hand across his bloodied lips, he watched Smoke with frightened eyes.

Smoke strode around the table. "Get up, you pup!"

Delaney shook his head.

Smoke planted a kick in his ribs. "Get up!"

Delaney snaked back. "No," he whimpered.

"There's only one way to settle this," said Smoke, dragging the kid to his feet by his silk shirt front. "That's guns!"

"No," whimpered Delaney.

"Take him into the back room and get him a Texas!" said Smoke to Lush.

Lush dragged Delaney away. There was something degrading in watching a man break down and quit the way Delaney had done.

Smoke was very big about it. Before the kid had gone two steps, Smoke picked up the bills from the table and thrust them contemptuously at the kid. Delaney took them.

In the back room of the saloon, Lush broke out a gun and holster. Delaney had caved into himself in a chair. He looked sick.

Lush, his contempt very real, thrust the belt at Delaney. "Put it on."

Delaney pushed it away.

"You can't run," said Lush. "You ain't got no hoss."

The kid stiffened. "What do you mean?"

"The bronc was hamstrung hours ago," said Lush.

"Hamstrung? Stardust?"

"Yeah."

Delaney caved into himself again and hid his face. His shoulders trembled and a sob caught in his throat.

Lush Wilson's lip curled. He shoved the gun at Delaney again. "If you're too yellah to even get mad about that, you better walk out there and die like a man anyhow. You'd be better off."

Consadine came in. He looked driven. "Listen, Delaney, I can call this off."

"Can you?" quivered the kid with sudden hope.

"Yeah," said Consadine. "You sign over the Rocking T on these papers here—I got them out of your saddlebags—and I'll see that Smoke leaves you alone."

The kid stared at the papers. "No! I can't do that!"

"Better to be broke than dead. Even killers don't stand any chance against Smoke Lassiter."

"I can't!" wept Delaney. "I . . . you don't understand. The sixty-five thousand . . ."

"Sign!" said Consadine, pushing a pen at him.

Suddenly Delaney's face was still. There was no hope anywhere in him. He looked long at the pen and then reached out—for the gun which Lush Wilson still held.

Wilson and Consadine exchanged a wondering glance.

Delaney stood up shakily. He clumsily buckled the belt about him.

"Look here, kid, there ain't any reason to die. Just sign . . ."

"You don't understand," said Delaney in a still voice. "If I die, the sixty-five thousand goes to—"

"Your mother," finished Wilson.

The kid finished fastening the gun belt. "I'll meet him. I can't do anything else. Go tell him I'll meet him in the street."

The first pearl of dawn was in the sky, graying the dirty window of the back room.

Consadine went out. Presently Smoke came back.

"Look here, kid," said Smoke, "if you'll sign, I'll call it off."

"I can't," said Delaney miserably.

"You know what happens to anybody that got to stand up to me," said Smoke. "You better sign, kid."

"No," shuddered Delaney.

He would not say more than that, no matter how much they pounded him. And at long last, Smoke lost his temper.

"Damn you for a fool!" yelled Smoke. "By God, I'll blow you apart! Come on outside!"

Consadine tried to stay Lassiter. But Delaney's obstinacy had taken the gunman past reason.

Lush Wilson pushed Delaney before him.

It was light in the street with the sun but a few minutes above the rim. The town had heard and the town had collected along the walks.

Head down, eyes upon the dusty street, the kid shuffled to its center.

Smoke, jaw tight set and eyes blazing, confronted him. "This is a joke on you," he said.

Delaney glanced up.

Smoke pulled the card from his pocket and shoved it under the kid's nose. "Runnin' away never helped none. You walked into the same thing all over again."

Delaney didn't care for the gunman's philosophy. "No," he said miserably. "It's no good to run away."

Smoke shoved the card back into his pocket. "Yeah, the joke's on you. Lush! We'll do this in style. You count twenty paces, and on your word *fire,* we'll turn and shoot."

Lush nodded.

Delaney and Smoke stood back to back in the dusty street. The sun was to be behind Smoke and in Delaney's eyes. Delaney did not protest. He stood very still.

"One," said Lush and the two men took the pace. "Two, three, four, five, six, seven, eight, nine, ten . . ." Delaney was walking like an animated doll. "Eleven, twelve, thirteen, fourteen . . ." The town watched as though hypnotized. "Fifteen, sixteen, seventeen, eighteen, nineteen, twenty!" The two men stood still, facing away from each other, forty paces of bright dawn air between them.

"FIRE!" shouted Lush.

Delaney did an about-face.

Smoke whirled, drawing as he turned. He started the downchop with his Texas.

Delaney was standing very straight. He held his revolver out from his shoulder, sighting it.

The two reports were a second apart. White smoke swirled.

Suddenly Lush gasped.

Smoke Lassiter's bullet had been blasted into the sky. Smoke screamed a curse and slashed down again.

Delaney fired a second time and again Lassiter's shot went straight up. Delaney's next four bullets went in a blur.

Lassiter lost his hat. He grabbed for his belt but it came apart in his hands, shot through on each side. He snatched again, in agony, at his right ear.

He stood there shaking. His right hand was a mass of blood and there was a clean hole in the ear.

"Now get out of town," drawled Delaney, reloading calmly,

Delaney fired a second time and again Lassiter's shot went straight up. Delaney's next four bullets went in a blur.

just as though Lassiter had forgotten all about fighting. Lassiter had.

He looked at Delaney through the bright dawn. Suddenly he saw that he was alive. That was enough for Lassiter. He knew at last what he was up against. He sprinted for the livery stable as fast as his legs could carry him.

He came out in an instant, eyes dilated. "My horse is dead!"

Eddie dived out of sight.

"If somebody killed your horse because it happened to be in my horse's stall," called Delaney, "then walk!"

Smoke turned, not intending to wait for a second invitation. But he had not heard the oncoming roar of the stage and it almost ran him down. He leaped aside and then a face in the window caught and held his attention as though he had seen a ghost.

The stage stopped and out leaped Bab Thompson of the Rocking T.

"By God, son, you shore wasn't wastin' any time."

Delaney grinned as he shook the hand. All Faro stayed in their tracks gaping in wonder. This was all wrong. Old Bab Thompson had been run out of the country and wouldn't ever have the nerve to come back. But Old Bab wasn't the kind of guy to pick up with a kid like Delaney . . . but Delaney was all wrong, too. He had stood up there and shot with an accuracy greater than anyone had ever seen in Faro—had stood up against Smoke Lassiter without blinking an eye. . . .

Smoke was still up the street, bewildered at Bab's return and connection with this lead-slinging kid.

Old Bab turned and greeted the men who lined the

street. "Gents, I want you to meet my pal Jacques Duval, the greatest duelist New Orleans ever produced. He come here to do me a favor and shore he done it."

And now Smoke Lassiter really did gape. The town, staring with respect and awe at "Delaney," abruptly turned their attention to Smoke. And then the enormity of the practical joke came home to them and with one great gust of laughter they jarred Lassiter to his shred of a soul.

Smoke turned. He made haste to get beyond the range of that bellow. But no matter how far he ran, he could still hear it behind him.

And for the next twenty years, Smoke Lassiter would still be listening to it.

Silent Pards

Chapter One

GOLD!

There could be no doubt about it.

The bared vein of jewelry rock was shot through with captured sunlight and the crumbling quartz was too feeble and old to retain its riches.

Once more Cherokee sank his sample pick into the lode, and dust and quartz and metal cascaded into his work-hardened old hand. He forgot, in that moment, that he had slogged for a heartbreaking month up this stream, that he had suffered from lack of food and the rheumatism which came on from the cold border nights. He forgot all his weariness. Indeed, the feel of the soft and glowing metal acted like a magic elixir upon him.

Pan, pan, pan, test, test, test. Mile upon rugged, dangerous mile. The sand had always yielded more and more in concentration until now, spotting this lode as the source, Cherokee stood with an easy old age in his palm.

Hardtack, his energetic shepherd dog, was hopefully rooting out a lizard when he heard his master talking to himself. The dog came skidding down the bank and romped up to the old prospector.

Cherokee might be termed a desert rat, his battered

sombrero may have been greasy and stained, his red shirt might have been missing most of its buttons and his boots may have been muddy, but Zeus never looked half so good to a Greek as Cherokee did to Hardtack.

The old man's face wreathed into a happy smile which spread his graying beard apart. "Hardtack, you see this?"

Hardtack sniffed at the handful of dirt and metal and decided it wasn't good to eat. Nevertheless he grinned dog-fashion and wagged his tail attentively, mutely saying, "Yes, yes, do go on. Please do."

"Well, sir," expanded Cherokee, "this is gold. You seen the stuff before but never no lode like this. And it means plenty. No more livin' off of lizards, no more drinkin' alkali water, no more sweatin' and broilin' for you and me. We're goin' to go to Californy and get us a ranch and just sit fer a spell and eat ice cream. All I got to do is file and then sell and off we go."

Hardtack, caught by the tone, barked in excitement. Cherokee walked down the bank to the shade of a boulder where Joe, his moth-eaten burro, leaned sleepily, regretting the flies.

"Joe!" cried Cherokee. "Wake up, there. Look what I got!"

Joe opened his left eye with a great deal of trouble and gave the gold a bored stare. He sniffed at it, thinking it might soothe his cactus-sated palate, got a noseful of dust and sneezed violently. This served to wake him up.

"Joe, yore goin' to have wheat cakes for breakfast every morning, *with syrup*!" stated Cherokee. "An' yore goin' to have a red bridle with gold tassels to keep the flies off yore face. All we gotta do is show this to the minin' men and we're fixed for life. Five years we been hoping for this and now, doggone it, it's gone and happened!"

Hardtack skipped around him in a circle, barking. Joe scented something in the air and looked suddenly alert. But his gaze was on the rim of the canyon and his long ears bent in that direction. Almost angrily he looked at the dog as though bidding him stop his noise so that hearing was possible for other, more important things.

"An' I'll have red carpet slippers and a meer—a meers . . . I'll have a pipe big as my fist and ten pounds of 'baccy. . . ." He went on with his simple desires until Hardtack stopped him.

With abrupt ferocity, the dog charged up the bank, every hair standing on end. Joe headed around and faced in that direction. It took Cherokee a moment to shift his train of thought into less pleasant channels.

A foot jabbed out in a savage kick from behind a boulder and Hardtack was hurled into a back dive. As soon as he lit, stunned, he struggled up and again started the charge.

"Come back," said Cherokee with a sinking sensation in his stomach.

Hardtack came limping back and took his stand back of the old man's knee.

A moment later a head appeared above the rim of the ravine and a pair of gray, chilly eyes examined the old prospector. "Okay, Lefty."

Another man appeared and then, behind him, came two more.

The quartet strode down the bank, watchful for any hostile move the prospector might make.

The leader showed the signs of former prosperity but the rough country had taken its toll of his expensive clothes. He had the stamp of a gambler—the dead face, the alert eyes, the slender hands.

"I'm Barlow."

It evidently should have meant something to Cherokee, but it didn't. "Pleased to meetcha," he said hesitantly.

"Yeah?" said Barlow. "That's a good thing because I didn't think you would be. How is it, Lefty?"

Squat, greasy Lefty had been examining the lode. "Jewelry rock. Worth seventy-five thousand, more or less, to any syndicate."

"That's all I wanted to know," said Barlow. "Okay, old man. Just keep walking."

"Wait," said Cherokee in sudden understanding. "You can't do this to me. I've looked for that for months. I've spent years trying to make a decent strike. If I don't get it now I'll never be able to wangle another grubstake. You—"

"I ain't interested in your woes, desert rat. Just keep going. Lefty will be in Calexico days before you get there, in case you want to get hopeful."

"I'll get the law!" cried Cherokee.

"Yeah? And who'd believe a guy so desert-dizzy that he doesn't even know he's been followed for days. Next time, don't talk out loud."

Cherokee did something very foolish then. Rage took him up with the force of a tornado and hurled him into Barlow. But not one blow did he land. Cherokee was slammed to earth with an expert blow.

Rage took him up with the force of a tornado and hurled him into Barlow. But not one blow did he land. Cherokee was slammed to earth with an expert blow.

With a scream of anger, Hardtack threw himself into the fray, sailing like a fang-tipped javelin toward Barlow's throat. A boot knocked him out of the air and he rolled senselessly up against the boulder.

With the true philosophy of the burro, Joe took it all in. And he did not strike until Barlow came within range. Barlow went down, bruised by the small hoof. The man got up, swearing and ready to shoot.

But Barlow recalled himself in time. No true violence would serve here. This desert rat would never have money enough to sue, would never be believed. And his friends would wonder only if either his dog or his burro turned up missing.

Accordingly, Barlow, with leveled gun, stirred Cherokee into life. Hardtack came around and showed his fangs.

"Come on," said Cherokee, bitterly.

Hardtack followed him down the ravine with Joe bringing up the rear. Once Cherokee looked back. On the plateau, Lefty had mounted and was already Calexico bound.

"I . . . I guess you'll have to wait a while for them wheat cakes and hamburger." He couldn't say any more, marching dejectedly around the bend in the trail, well knowing his defenselessness against armed and ruthless men.

He had a chance to make another strike, but maybe not for years and years. And meantime, would he ever get another grubstake?

Chapter Two

IT required more than a month for Cherokee to recover from the loss of his bonanza and the shattering of his dreams. During that time, the Calexico storekeeper, Thompson, sturdily withheld the very necessary grubstake. But after the weeks of seeing Cherokee mope about the town, even Thompson's hard and commercial heart gave way and the bacon and beans were forthcoming.

"This is positively the last," stated Thompson. "And this time I hope you don't bring back no cock-and-bull story about claim jumpers. You got any idea where you're going?"

Cherokee gave a tug to his battered hat and gazed southward through the store's dirty window. "Remember Tulare Bill's pool? Well, I think maybe I'll slide over the line and just see about it."

"You can't cross the line!" stated Thompson. "The *rurales* would have your scalp in a week and your gold too."

But Cherokee was driven by desperation. "I guess I'll have to take that chance."

Thompson was anxious. He saw about two thousand dollars in invested groceries over the years walking into oblivion. "But they'll kill you, Cherokee!"

"I guess that's the worst they can do. Come on, Hardtack."

Thompson watched the trio growing small across the

shimmering wastes. Tulare Bill's rumored pool had failed to attract even braver souls than Cherokee despite its reported richness. But as Thompson at least had a chance of regaining his expenditures, he had to be content.

Southward traveled Cherokee into Mexico. Diligently, as the weeks went by, he searched for the three small peaks which triangulated Tulare Bill's long-lost find.

He saw nothing of the *rurales* and chalked it off to the fact that these illimitable plains could have held an army unsuspected.

The sun spun in the cloudless sky; the brassy sands and garish rocks pugnaciously hurled the heat skyward again. Water was scarce and once Cherokee traveled three days without filling his canteens. And it was like him to give more water to his dog and burro than he took himself.

And then, one hot twilight, he saw the three peaks. And seeing them he understood why they had been lost so long. Two of them were only peaks when viewed from this angle. Otherwise they were ridges all too common in this rough border country. That night he did not sleep, so anxious was he to search out the pool, so afraid that there would be no pool at all, but only Tulare Bill's rumor.

At dawn he started forth from his dry camp with Hardtack panting like a miniature steam engine at his side and with Joe slumberously trudging in their wake.

Joe it was who found the water. Suddenly his ears went up and he raised his head and tested the hot wind with his quivering nose. He began to trot ahead, passing Cherokee, sample pick clanging against mining pan on the load.

Joe soon found the pool. It was in a canyon of red sandstone which served as an effectual mask. It was fed by a subterranean stream which came to the surface here and only here and then vanished swiftly into the sand. The pool itself was about nine yards in diameter and the banks . . .

Cherokee gave a whoop and slid down the slope. The banks were black.

When he had slaked his thirst, he lost no time in making a test. And Tulare Bill had been right. This spot, evidently the remains of a lode which had been eroded in the ages past, yielded fifty dollars to the pan in rough nuggets.

Cherokee, working day after day, as long as there was light, could not believe his good fortune. Before he went to bed he would spend an hour or more pouring the yellow weight from hand to hand. To strike it twice within three months seemed to him a miracle and he forgot the weary, waterless desert days which had made his "miracle" possible.

He knew that he could not start to exhaust this place with a pan. A rocker box was what he needed but he had nothing with which to build one. The more he thought about it, the more certain he became that he should return to Calexico and get building material. A week's work had netted him eleven thousand dollars while if he had had a rocker box the take would have been triple that sum. Besides, Thompson had been sparing with his supplies this time and food was low.

Yes, he decided, he would have to return to Calexico. And wouldn't Thompson's eyes pop out when he saw this virgin gold!

Accordingly, the next morning, Cherokee packed up and started on his way. He had a few of the rarer specimens in a leather poke inside his shirt but most of his wealth was packed on Joe because of its extreme weight.

He had gone about a hundred yards away from his camp when a man in sombrero and serape stepped into the game trail before him. Both eye and white-toothed smile were bad.

"Buenos dias," said the *rural* officer.

Cherokee stopped and Joe bumped into his back. Hardtack stared with suspicion. Hardtack did not like Mexicans.

"You have been amusing yourself, *señor*?" said the stranger. "Perhaps by panning gold, yes?"

Cherokee caught movements on either side. Horsemen, still mounted, were motionless in the chaparral.

"I ain't got any gold," said Cherokee stolidly.

"Ah, now, *señor,* it is not good to lie. It is not godly. Have you no thought for the destination of your immortal soul?" Smiling, the officer approached Joe, whose ears went back. Hardtack hugged Cherokee's leg and growled.

The man stopped. "Very well, *señor,* then do me the favor of giving me your gold bags." His hand was carelessly upon his gun.

Cherokee wanted badly to resist. But he was unarmed and he well knew that he was very lucky to get off with his life. How easy it would be for them to shoot him. Indeed, all in all, this officer was being very courteous and kind.

At last Cherokee reluctantly turned and unfastened his bags of hard-won dust. Disgustedly he flung them to the officer.

With a sweeping bow, the *rural* stepped aside. “A pleasant journey, *señor.*”

Raging inwardly but calm without, Cherokee trudged northward across the scorching sand. At long last he looked at Hardtack. “The last grubstake,” he sighed. “And how’ll I ever get the nerve to tell Thompson?”

Chapter Three

IT was evening and Calexico was celebrating the departure of the day's heat by risking their money and wetting their whistles in the Oasis. Thompson leaned against the bar nursing a drink and staring at the puddle of wasted liquor under it with a scowling brow.

Behind him a trio of voices rose to obliterate lesser throats and Thompson turned to see that two comparative newcomers to Calexico—namely Lefty and Barlow—were disagreeing with the faro dealer in no uncertain terms.

Without too much interest Thompson listened to the complaints.

Finally, Barlow, not wanting to make a fight of it in view of the bouncer and proprietor who were approaching, pushed back with an angry gesture and stalked toward the door.

"That was my last cent," snarled Barlow.

"Geez, it didn't take you long to drop twenty grand," said Lefty.

"It lasted two months, didn't it?" snapped Barlow. "But what the hell? There's plenty more easy money kicking around." Suddenly he stopped and drew back from the door. Lefty stared into the darkness and then he too backed up. They leaned against the wall as though they had noticed nothing.

Outside, Cherokee disconsolately told Joe to wait for him

and then he and Hardtack walked up the steps and into the saloon. The sudden light was apparently too much for Cherokee's sun-abused eyes as he stopped uncertainly just inside and looked all around. As the old man's gaze passed over them, both Barlow and Lefty flinched but Cherokee, squinting, walked deeper into the saloon. At last the old man saw Thompson at the bar.

Thompson, beholding his debtor, straightened up with sudden hope. There was a nicety about such things and Cherokee did not look too down in the mouth.

"Hello, Cherokee," said Thompson. "Have a drink."

"Don't mind if I do," said the prospector. He poured it out and put it down.

"Have another," said Thompson, bursting with his question.

Cherokee had another and shuddered it into a more comfortable spot in his midriff. He wiped his hand across his mouth. It was suddenly apparent that the two drinks had hit bottom with a splash. Having abstained for many weeks and being empty, it was not strange that Cherokee began to glow.

He fished into his shirt and pulled out the poke, clumsily untying the strings. He poured the specimens he had retained into Thompson's hand.

"Ain't they beauties?" said Cherokee.

Thompson avidly examined them. But he was a wise mining man in his own right and in these nuggets he beheld what was obviously the pick of a take. One, for instance, was wire gold, a typical prospector's keepsake.

"There's more?" demanded Thompson.

Cherokee hedged but only for an instant. "Shore."

"You wouldn't be showing me this just to get another grubstake, would you?"

Cherokee's blue eyes were the soul of innocence. "Me? Why, I ain't never lied to you, Thompson. Now have I?"

"Well, what's the story?" said Thompson.

"I run out of grub, that was all. Just as I found these, I run out of grub. And I need a rocker box. There's plenty more where these come from." Quite obviously the old man was thinking fast.

"Maybe I'm a fool to believe you. Maybe you've kept these nuggets around for years. They ain't worth fifty dollars all told. Any dust?"

"Well . . . I didn't have time. . . . Look, Mr. Thompson, all I need is a rocker box and a grubstake and I'll bring back a hundred thousand dollars' worth of gold. I found Tulare Bill's pool!"

Thompson was alarmed at the loudness with which whiskey made the old man speak. "Look, you come around to my store in the morning and I'll give you your grubstake. But so help me, if you're wrong this time, you can starve to death for all of me!"

Cherokee began to breathe more easily. Most of the tiredness had gone out of him and there was a hint of swagger as he marched through the door.

He gave Joe a playful tap on the nose and Hardtack frisked in a circle and barked.

"I dunno where we'll head for, pardners," said Cherokee,

"but we can't go south. Never you mind, though. Twice we struck it and we'll do it again. There's a place over by Wolf Spring I thought maybe—"

"You ain't goin' to Wolf Spring, old-timer," said a soft voice behind him. "You're takin' us to the place you got them nuggets."

Cherokee whirled and beheld Barlow. Hardtack snarled.

"Just keep walkin'," said Barlow. "Our shack's down at the end of the street. Lefty, get Sam and Tex. We're leavin' before dawn."

"You can't do this!" wailed Cherokee, staring up at the tall Barlow. "You can't! I wangled another chance. I got to make good this time. I'll starve to death if I don't!"

"You found Tulare Bill's pool," said Barlow. "It ain't goin' to get lost again."

Fuming, Cherokee was marched to the shack and was shoved inside. "I ain't goin' to do this!" he protested.

"You will if you want to keep livin'."

"But . . . but . . . what'll you do with me if I take you there?"

"Let you go if you play straight with us. Might even cut you in. Now sit down and take it easy before I knock you down."

Sam and Tex entered. Barlow turned over the guard to them. With a final grin at Cherokee, Barlow went out.

Lefty was nervous. "We can't do this," said Lefty, jerking his thumb at the shack. "It's kidnaping. He's bound to talk. Nobody listened the first time but if he turns up with another yarn about us maybe they'll investigate. That storekeeper knows we must have heard him."

"Forget it," said Barlow with a grin. "You think I'm that dumb? When we clean up that pool, there ain't nobody goin' to object."

"I get it," said Lefty.

Chapter Four

SIX weeks later, Cherokee, gaunt on starvation rations, knew that he had reached his last day on the rocker box. He released the handle and fingered the riffles hopelessly.

"Get busy," said Barlow, who sat in the shade with a rifle across his knees.

Cherokee looked up. "Not much use to keep going. We've been out of the pocket for two days."

Sam wandered over and made a test with a mining pan. Tex, who had been shoveling, leaned upon his implement and heaved a sigh.

"I hopes that's the last," said Tex. "I'm sick to death of this damned place."

Barlow examined the goldless sand. "Yeah, the old coot's right. Not even any colors now. Guess we've got it all, boys."

Lefty grinned and glanced toward the camp on the edge of the pool. There in plain sight were piled the fat pokes. "It's all right with me. We get about twenty-five apiece this trip."

"We can make that spring to the north if we leave now," said Barlow. "I'm itchin' to start spendin' and it's Frisco this trip. No more Calexico for me. Start loadin' up, Sam. You, Lefty, put the take on two burros and to hell with the shovels."

From sheer weariness, old Cherokee sat down on the bank and buried his face in his arms. He was dimly aware of their activities and then, at long last, he realized that they were finished.

Barlow's boot stirred him.

"Come on over here on the flat," said Barlow.

With a start Cherokee saw the gun's glitter matched Barlow's cold eyes. "What you goin' to do with me?"

"Think we'll let you run around shootin' off your face this time? We let you off once. Twice is too much to ask of anybody."

"Wait," said Cherokee anxiously. "I didn't do nothin'. I dug like you told me. I got out my share of this gold. You can at least—"

"Quit it," said Barlow. "You're breakin' my heart."

"Somebody'll find me," said Cherokee. "The Mexicans come to this water hole and if I got a bullet in me, it'll get around."

Barlow thought that over, clearly puzzled. Lefty came up.

"What are you waitin' for?" said Lefty.

"The old coot's right," said Barlow. "A bullet would mark him up and I'm damned if I'll spend the time buryin' him."

Lefty reached into his pocket and brought forth a wad of rawhide thongs.

Cherokee protested anew, aghast at being left to fry, but Lefty and Barlow were too much for him and with swift and efficient hands they trussed him up with the thongs.

"Lefty," said Barlow, jerking his thumb toward the flat above the pool.

Lefty halfheartedly yanked Cherokee to his feet.

"What you goin' to do with me?" said Cherokee.

Neither one answered him. Lefty drew his gun and prodded

Cherokee forward. The old prospector walked stiffly and Lefty, following after, glanced a couple times back at Barlow.

They arrived at the flat. Sam and Tex and Barlow were all watching. Suddenly Lefty stood back and shoved his gun at Sam.

"Murder ain't in my line," said Lefty. "I ain't runnin' no chance if you guys should happen to open up."

Sam looked at the revolver but he did not offer to take it.

"What the hell's the matter with you?" snarled Barlow, striding up.

"If you want him killed, kill him yourself!" stated Lefty.

Barlow saw that his blustering was not going to work and he, too, failed to take the gun from Lefty. Murder was, after all, murder.

Finally, in disgust, Barlow tramped over to the packs and got a length of rawhide riata. He came back.

"You ain't goin' to do that to me!" wailed Cherokee.

Barlow struck him and knocked him flat. Cherokee vainly fought back but with Lefty's help, Barlow finally trussed the old man until his heels were almost meeting the back of his neck.

"He won't get out of that," said Barlow. "And he won't be marked up with no bullet holes neither. String those burros out, you guys. We'll cross the sink by moonlight and be in Calexico in three days."

Miserably Cherokee watched them get the burros into line.

Because, unlike the others, he had never been trained to follow, Joe was in the lead. Once, somewhat puzzled, Joe looked back at his master who lay beside the pool. But a stick cracked on Joe's rump and he started off, staggering a little under his weight of dust, with the others coming after.

Hardtack skipped after Joe and then, when the train began to file up toward the canyon rim, looked back at Cherokee and saw that the old man was not following. Uncertainly, Hardtack went back to his master, glancing now and then toward the departing train.

Worried, Hardtack walked around Cherokee, failing to understand what was wrong. He whined and licked Cherokee's face.

"It's all right, fellow," said Cherokee. "If you know what's good for you, you better follow Joe. You'll starve here."

Hardtack knew the order and he started to carry it out. But when he reached the bottom of the incline he stopped and, with paw upraised, looked back at Cherokee. Finally he returned and lay down beside the old prospector.

"You damned fool," said Cherokee, hiding the fact that he was choked with emotion.

Joe's bell tinkled out into silence. Hardtack whined once in a while but he kept his vigil.

"I didn't think they'd do this to me," said Cherokee again and again.

And the shadows of evening grew longer and longer. At long last came the sound for which Cherokee had been waiting. The rifle shot was faint with distance but the sudden explosive volume of others began to drum like summer thunder up in the canyons.

Hardtack raised his head in wonder and gazed toward

the sound. To him gunfire meant rabbit hunting in the days before the lock on Cherokee's gun had been broken.

Cherokee began to worm himself down the bank. Presently he began to slip faster and then, with a splash, he fell into the shallow, chilly pool.

"Hardtack!" cried Cherokee. "Go bring Joe here. Understand? Bring Joe here!"

Hardtack liked that command better, although he was still puzzled by his master's position in the pool. The command was well known to him and it meant that he would be coming back. And so, with relief, he romped up the incline and out of sight through the twilight of evening.

It was hard for Cherokee to keep his head out of water but he knew what he was doing. At long last he felt the soaked rawhide begin to stretch and, finally, he was able to work one wrist out of the confining bond. Once that hand was free from the now greasy and limp leather, he quickly freed his legs.

The gunfire was still going strong in the exact spot where Cherokee himself had been ambushed. There, he knew, the canyon pinched out to the flat and, from the length of time the fight had gone on, at least one or two of the claim jumpers were holding that canyon entrance. Of course the burros would still be in the canyon, behind their defenders—but that was up to Hardtack.

Cherokee floundered up the bank, water streaming from him. For a few minutes he was very anxious and then, with a chuckle of relief, he heard a tinkling bell on the incline.

Hardtack, tail wagging, came into sight with Joe's lead

rope firmly in his teeth, feeling very superior to the burro who followed him with so little thought.

And behind Joe came the other animals, all faithfully following from force of habit.

Cherokee lost no time. He took the lead rope from Hardtack and swiftly led the way down the ravine toward another incline which led up and to the west.

They traveled very fast and never once looked back through the darkness. Their tracks were masked by the hard rock over which they traveled.

On this circuitous course, Cherokee knew they would need an extra day to get to Calexico. But that was all right. The point was to get to Calexico on a route where they could not be stopped.

He had had that route figured out for a long, long time in just such an event as this.

Sound carried far through the desert night.

Miles behind them guns were still going and *rurales* and Barlow's men were still blasting each other to oblivion.

With a shout of laughter, Cherokee forged ahead.

Story Preview

Story Preview

NOW that you've just ventured through some of the captivating tales in the Stories from the Golden Age collection by L. Ron Hubbard, turn the page and enjoy a preview of *The Magic Quirt*. Join Old Laramie, cook for the Lazy G Ranch and holder of a silver quirt recently given to him after he saves an Aztec family from bandits. The quirt's magical properties allow Laramie to begin performing extraordinary deeds of courage—or does it?

The Magic Quirt

"YE'RE powerless! With the magic wave of my left paw I creates you a statue! With a quick thumbin' of my right, I creates you a corpse!"

BANG! BLOWIE!

But it wasn't Old Laramie's imaginary gun. It was a real, honest-to-gosh shootin' iron. And Bessie and Mac recognized it as such, reared against the remorseless weight of the unbraked wagon, got shoved ahead, reared again and then, bronc fashion, scared to death, lit out like the Cannonball Stage straight down the curving road.

Whoever it was that had shot was not in sight. The road's curve hid him. But the speed with which Old Laramie was traveling would very shortly remedy that.

His old slouch hat whipped back in the hurricane and the chin thong nearly strangled him. He tried to grind home the brake shoe but he missed and had to use both hands and both feet to hold on. The reins were loosely tied to the brake and to reach them was impossible. He couldn't reach his rabbit's foot and his Little Jim Dandy Guaranteed Lucky Ring was carelessly left in camp!

Old Laramie once upon a time had been as tough as the next one, but three bullet holes, a sense of defeat and old age had ended that. He screamed like a wounded mountain lion and the scenery blurred by.

The chuck wagon finished the curve on two wheels, swapped to the other two, came back and tried to lean over the hundred-foot drop into the dry arroyo.

Straight ahead were six pack animals, clinging to the cliff beside the road as only burros can do. Directly in the track of the plunging wagon were two mounted men, holding guns on somebody or something out of Old Laramie's view.

But the horsemen weren't there long. They gave a white-eyed look at the cometing wagon and dug spur. Their outraged mounts reared and fought, to break away down the road in an uncontrolled run. The riders were out of sight and still going an instant later when Mac, tangling with a sideswiped burro, upset the chuck wagon entire, flat and loud in the middle of the road.

Old Laramie floated to an easy landing in sand and sagebrush. The sound of breaking crockery gradually ceased to echo in the surrounding arroyos. The dust dropped slowly down in the dusk.

Old Laramie spat, sat up, felt of his bones and then swore luridly and long. That seemed to relieve him somewhat and he looked at his horses. They were bruised but had struggled to their feet with no bones broken. The chuck wagon, however, had spilled everything from frying pans to cockroaches.

"*¡Ah, gracias, gracias!*" wailed somebody. "*¡Gracias, amigo! ¡Gracias infinitas para todos mandados!*"

Old Laramie understood very little Spanish but he knew

he was being thanked and he turned to find a small, fat Indian from over the line waddling up, bowing and advancing.

Three small children now rose wide-eyed from the sage and a woman, as fat as her man, came off a rock above the trail carrying a fourth child.

It was a very strange thing, thought Old Laramie. Sure these Mexican Indians didn't seem to be good bait for the owl-hoots.

The flood of Spanish went on with much flinging of the arms, and when it seemed that he was about to get kissed by the woman, Laramie got gruff.

"Hell, wasn't nothin'! Gimme a hand with this yere wagon."

They gave him a hand. The three kids picked up groceries and pans while the man and his wife aided to rig a block and tackle to right the wagon.

It was quite dark when the task was done and Laramie, less breakage, was ready to proceed on his way. He was getting mighty anxious when he thought of how Lee Jacoby would take this. For he should have been at Camp Seven something before supper time.

The little Indian was jabbering with more thanks.

"Quit it," said Laramie. "I would've done it for anybody. But just now I got to go."

"¡Señor, su pago!"

"Pago yourself," said Old Laramie genially. "But I got to go. I'm goin' to be roasted, clothes, hoofs and hide, as it is!"

The Indian was pulling forth a fat sack. From it he poured a small torrent of silver and gold coins. Laramie's eyes popped.

So that was the bait! But he found that he was about to be paid. This unsettled him.

"Dang it, you ornery little cactus-eater. I didn't do you no favor on purpose. My horses run away and . . ."

The Indian tried to push the money at him but he finally succeeded in pushing it back. There was an immediate conference between the Mexican and his wife and finally the man went to the sad little burros and dug into a pack.

The thing which he now extended to Laramie glittered in the starlight. And the man made a valiant attempt at English.

"See! Thees theeng. *Látigo.* Make beeg man. *Muy fuerte* man, *látigo* he take. Beeg man make. *Muy fuerte.* Me not Indian. Me Aztec. You savvy? You keep. You beeg, beeg man. *Mucho* lucky. *Mucho!*"

Puzzled, Laramie took the object and found it to be a silver-mounted quirt. He was too anxious to get to Camp Seven to delay and so, saluting with the quirt, hastily got started before the thanks began again.

Mac and Bessie picked their way amongst the rocks of the canyon and soon came out on the flat where, in the distance, a fire marked the whereabouts of Camp Seven.

Glossary

STORIES FROM THE GOLDEN AGE *reflect the words and expressions used in the 1930s and 1940s, adding unique flavor and authenticity to the tales. While a character's speech may often reflect regional origins, it also can convey attitudes common in the day. So that readers can better grasp such cultural and historical terms, uncommon words or expressions of the era, the following glossary has been provided.*

---

agates: gemstones with colorful concentric ringlike bands that sometimes look like eyes.

alkali: a powdery white mineral that salts the ground in many low places in the West. It whitens the ground where water has risen to the surface and gone back down.

Arizona Rangers: a group of mounted lawmen organized in 1901 to protect the Arizona Territory from outlaws and rustlers so that the Territory could apply for statehood. They were picked from officers, military men, ranchers and cowboys. With maximum company strength of 26 men, they covered the entire territory. By 1909, the Arizona Rangers had largely accomplished their goals and were disbanded by the Territorial Governor. In total there were only 107 original Territorial Rangers.

arroyo: (chiefly in southwestern US) a small, steep-sided watercourse or gulch with a nearly flat floor, usually dry except after heavy rains.

'baccy: tobacco; the leaves of the tobacco plant dried and prepared for smoking or chewing.

batwings: long chaps (leather leggings the cowboy wears to protect his legs) with big flaps of leather. They usually fasten with rings and snaps.

black: black sand; a heavy, glossy, partly magnetic mixture of fine sands. Black sand is an indicator of the presence of gold or other precious metals.

blue: a poker chip having a high value.

bonanza: in mining, a rich mine or vein of silver or gold; anything that is a mine of wealth or yields a large income.

buffaloed: deceived; caused to accept what is false, especially by trickery or misrepresentation.

caballeros: (Spanish) gentlemen.

Calexico: a city in Southern California on the US-Mexican border. Founded in 1899, it is a coined name combining the words *California* and *Mexico*.

Californio: of a Californian, or one of the original Spanish colonists of California or their descendants.

Cannonball Stage: Cannonball Express; in 1901, the Cannonball Stage was started and continued to run until about 1913. It used six horses rather than four, and carried the mail as well as passengers. The Cannonball earned its name by "shooting" seventy-two miles in twelve hours, considered terrific speed in those days, with stops every ten miles for fresh horses.

chaparral: small, shrubby trees native to the dry soils of North America, such as scrub oak, mesquite, vines and any sort of shrubbery all tangled together. They can be found in patches or covering a plain.

chuck wagon: a mess wagon of the cow country. It is usually made by fitting, at the back end of an ordinary farm wagon, a large box that contains shelves and has a hinged lid fitted with legs that serves as a table when lowered. The chuck wagon is a cowboy's home on the range, where he keeps his bedroll and dry clothes, gets his food and has a warm fire.

coat of mail: chain mail; flexible armor made of joined metal links.

cockleburs: any of several weeds having small seedlike fruits enclosed within a prickly bur that clings readily to clothing or animal fur.

Colt: a single-action, six-shot cylinder revolver, most commonly available in .45- or .44-caliber versions. It was first manufactured in 1873 for the Army by the Colt Firearms Company, the armory founded by American inventor Samuel Colt (1814–1862) who revolutionized the firearms industry with the invention of the revolver. The Colt, also known as the Peacemaker, was also made available to civilians. As a reliable, inexpensive and popular handgun among cowboys, it became known as the "cowboy's gun" and a symbol of the Old West.

concha: a disk, traditionally of hammered silver and resembling a shell or flower, used as a decoration piece on belts, harnesses, etc.

cow town: a town at the end of the trail from which cattle were shipped; later applied to towns in the cattle country that depended upon the cowman and his trade for their existence.

coyote: used for a man who has the sneaking and skulking characteristics of a coyote.

'dobe: short for adobe; a building constructed with sun-dried bricks made from clay.

double eagle: a gold coin of the US with a denomination of twenty dollars, produced from 1850 to 1933. Prior to 1850, eagles with a denomination of ten dollars were the largest denomination of US coin, and since the twenty-dollar gold piece had twice the value of the eagle, it was designated a "double eagle."

down in the mouth: dejected; depressed; disheartened.

dragged: drawn; taken or obtained (money, salary) from a source of supply.

faro: a gambling game played with cards and popular in the American West of the nineteenth century. In faro, the players bet on the order in which the cards will be turned over by the dealer. The cards were kept in a dealing box to keep track of the play.

filler: fill; in a card game, drawing the last card needed to make a five-card hand, such as a straight, flush or full house.

forty-one or **.41:** Derringer .41-caliber short pistol. Named for the US gunsmith Henry Deringer (1786–1868), who designed it.

Franciscan: a member of a religious order founded by St. Francis in 1209. The Franciscans were dedicated to the virtues of humility and poverty.

Frisco: San Francisco.

G-men: government men; agents of the Federal Bureau of Investigation.

¡Gracias, amigo! ¡Gracias infinitas para todos mandados!: (Spanish) Thanks, friend! Infinite thanks for all you have sent us!

grubstake: supplies or funds furnished a mining prospector on promise of a share in his discoveries.

hamstrung: said of a horse that has had its hamstring, the large tendon above the back of the hock, severed thereby rendering it unable to control its legs.

Henry: the first rifle to use a cartridge with a metallic casing rather than the undependable, self-contained powder, ball and primer of previous rifles. It was named after B. Tyler Henry, who designed the rifle and the cartridge.

holdout: playing cards hidden in a gambling game for the purpose of cheating.

hole card: the card dealt face down in the first round of a deal in stud poker.

hoss: horse.

iron: a handgun, especially a revolver.

Jesuits: Catholic order of clergy called The Society of Jesus. Founded by Ignatius Loyola in 1534, it was committed to education, theological scholarship and missionary work.

jewelry rock: gold-bearing vein quartz.

jingle bob: make sounds from the little pear-shaped pendants hanging loosely from the end of a spur (small spiked wheel attached to the heel of a rider's boot); their sole function is to make music.

látigo: (Spanish) whip.

light out or **lit out:** to leave quickly; depart hurriedly.

lily-livered: lacking courage; cowardly. Originating from the whiteness of the lily flower and from the former belief that anger depended on the body producing large quantities of yellow bile, thus a white liver meant a lack of courage.

lit: landed.

livery stable: a stable that accommodates and looks after horses for their owners.

lock: the mechanism by which the charge or cartridge of a firearm is exploded.

lode: a deposit of ore that fills a fissure in a rock, or a vein of ore deposited between layers of rock.

meers: meerschaum pipe; a smoking pipe made from meerschaum, a white mineral deposit.

mesquite: any of several small spiny trees or shrubs native to the southwestern US and Mexico, and used for forage for cattle amongst other things.

muy fuerte: (Spanish) very strong.

"'O Sole Mio": a universally famous song written in 1898. Because the song is so well known, many hotels and restaurants have been named after it. In Italian, it translates literally to "I have my sun."

Overland: Overland Stage; stagecoach line in the mid-nineteenth century that transported mail and passengers.

owl-hoot: outlaw.

Peacemaker: nickname for the single-action (that is, cocked by hand for each shot), six-shot Army model revolver first produced in 1873 by the Colt Firearms Company, the armory founded by Samuel Colt (1814–1862). The handgun of the Old West, it became the instrument of both lawmaker and lawbreaker during the last twenty-five years of the nineteenth century. It soon earned various names, such as "hog leg," "Equalizer," and "Judge Colt and his jury of six."

penny-ante: small-time.

poke: a small sack or bag, usually a crude leather pouch, in which a miner carried his gold dust and nuggets.

pulling leather: grabbing onto the saddle while riding a bucking horse. It shows a lack of skill or courage, or both. A cowboy hates to have to grab the saddle horn to stay on, and most will allow themselves to be thrown off before they will pull leather.

punch cows: to take care of cows; to drive cows; to be a cowpuncher, a hired hand who tends cattle.

puncher: a hired hand who tends cattle and performs other duties on horseback.

quartz: a common, hard mineral, often with brilliant crystals. It is generally found in large masses or veins, and mined for its gold content.

quirt: a riding whip with a short handle and a braided leather lash.

rapier: a small sword, especially of the eighteenth century, having a narrow blade and used for thrusting.

riata: a long noosed rope used to catch animals.

riffles: in mining, the strips of metal or wooden slats fixed to the bottom of a rocker box or sluice (a long sloping trough into which water is directed), that run perpendicular to the flow of water. The weight of the gold causes it to sink, where it is captured by these riffles.

rocker box: a rectangular wooden box set on rockers. The rocking motion causes the mixture of dirt and water to flow through the box, with gold-bearing particles trapped by riffles on the bottom.

rootity-tootinest: from rootin'-tootin'; noisiest, most rambunctious.

run-over: of boots, where the heel is so unevenly worn on the outside that the back of the boot starts to lean to one side and does not sit straight above the heel.

rurales: (Spanish) Mexican Rural Guard, a force of mounted police. They wore a distinctive gray uniform braided in silver, a wide sombrero and red or black necktie. Their roles paralleled the Texas Rangers.

saddle tramp: a professional chuck-line (food-line) rider; anyone who is out of a job and riding through the country. Any worthy cowboy may be forced to ride chuck-line at certain seasons, but the professional chuck-line rider is just a plain range bum, despised by all cowboys. He is one who takes advantage of the country's hospitality and stays as long as he dares wherever there is no work for him to do and the meals are free and regular.

Scheherazade: the female narrator of *The Arabian Nights,* who during one thousand and one adventurous nights saved her life by entertaining her husband, the king, with stories.

scourge: somebody or something that is perceived as an agent of punishment, destruction or severe criticism.

¡Señor, su pago!: (Spanish) Sir, your payment!

serape: a long, brightly colored woolen blanket worn as a cloak by some men from Mexico, Central America and South America.

sink: a depression in the land surface where water has no outlet and simply stands. The word is usually applied to dry lake beds, where the evaporating water has left alkali and other mineral salts.

sky-hooter: hoot owl; a night owl; a nocturnal bird of prey. Used figuratively.

slouch hat: a wide-brimmed felt hat with a chinstrap.

sombrero: a Mexican style of hat that was common in the Southwest. It had a high-curved wide brim, a long, loose chin strap and the crown was dented at the top. Like cowboy hats generally, it kept off the sun and rain, fended off the branches and served as a handy bucket or cup.

sorrel: a horse with a reddish-brown coat.

Stetson: as the most popular broad-brimmed hat in the West, it became the generic name for *hat.* John B. Stetson was a master hat maker and founder of the company that has been making Stetsons since 1865. Not only can the Stetson stand up to a terrific amount of beating, the cowboy's hat has more different uses than any other garment he wears. It keeps the sun out of the eyes and off the neck; it serves as an umbrella; it makes a great fan, which sometimes is needed when building a fire or shunting cattle about; the brim serves as a cup to water oneself, or as a bucket to water the horse or put out the fire.

stone hotel: a prison.

stud: stud poker; a game of poker in which the first round of cards is dealt face down, and the others face up.

St. Vitus: St. Vitus' dance; a nervous disorder causing involuntary rapid movements likened to dancing.

Texas: a .44- or .36-caliber revolver, made by Clark, Sherrard & Co. During the Civil War, they made a contract with the State of Texas to deliver these revolvers, intended for the Confederacy. More Texas revolvers were sold out the back door, for more money, than those delivered to the state. The name "Clark, Sherrard & Co/Lancaster Texas" is prominently stamped onto the barrel of the gun.

thirteen steps: gallows; traditionally, there are thirteen steps leading up to a gallows.

tinhorn: someone, especially a gambler, who pretends to be important, but actually has little money, influence or skill.

Uncle Sam: the cartoon embodiment of the government of the United States of America beginning in the first part of the nineteenth century. The initials US, of Uncle Sam, were also taken to stand for "United States."

whippersnapper: an impertinent young person, usually a young man, who lacks proper respect for the older generation; a youngster with an excess of both ambition and impertinence.

white feather: a single white feather is a symbol of cowardice. It comes from cockfighting, and the belief that a gamecock sporting a white feather in its tail is not a purebred and is likely to be a poor fighter.

Winchester: an early family of repeating rifles; a single-barreled rifle containing multiple rounds of ammunition. Manufactured by the Winchester Repeating Arms Company, it was widely used in the US during the latter half of the nineteenth century. The 1873 model is often called "the gun that won the West" for its immense popularity at that time, as well as its use in fictional Westerns.

wire gold: gold ore that looks like its description: fine, short pieces of wire, or a tangled wirelike mass. It is found mostly in pockets or veins.

yahoo: degraded or bestial person. "Yahoo" is a name invented by Jonathan Swift in *Gulliver's Travels* for an imaginary race of brutes having the form of men.

L. Ron Hubbard in the Golden Age of Pulp Fiction

In writing an adventure story
a writer has to know that he is adventuring
for a lot of people who cannot.
The writer has to take them here and there
about the globe and show them
excitement and love and realism.
As long as that writer is living the part of an
adventurer when he is hammering
the keys, he is succeeding with his story.

Adventuring is a state of mind.
If you adventure through life, you have a
good chance to be a success on paper.

Adventure doesn't mean globe-trotting,
exactly, and it doesn't mean great deeds.
Adventuring is like art.
You have to live it to make it real.

—L. RON HUBBARD

L. Ron Hubbard and American Pulp Fiction

BORN March 13, 1911, L. Ron Hubbard lived a life at least as expansive as the stories with which he enthralled a hundred million readers through a fifty-year career.

Originally hailing from Tilden, Nebraska, he spent his formative years in a classically rugged Montana, replete with the cowpunchers, lawmen and desperadoes who would later people his Wild West adventures. And lest anyone imagine those adventures were drawn from vicarious experience, he was not only breaking broncs at a tender age, he was also among the few whites ever admitted into Blackfoot society as a bona fide blood brother. While if only to round out an otherwise rough and tumble youth, his mother was that rarity of her time—a thoroughly educated woman—who introduced her son to the classics of Occidental literature even before his seventh birthday.

But as any dedicated L. Ron Hubbard reader will attest, his world extended far beyond Montana. In point of fact, and as the son of a United States naval officer, by the age of eighteen he had traveled over a quarter of a million miles. Included therein were three Pacific crossings to a then still mysterious Asia, where he ran with the likes of Her British Majesty's agent-in-place

L. Ron Hubbard, left, at Congressional Airport, Washington, DC, 1931, with members of George Washington University flying club.

for North China, and the last in the line of Royal Magicians from the court of Kublai Khan. For the record, L. Ron Hubbard was also among the first Westerners to gain admittance to forbidden Tibetan monasteries below Manchuria, and his photographs of China's Great Wall long graced American geography texts.

Upon his return to the United States and a hasty completion of his interrupted high school education, the young Ron Hubbard entered George Washington University. There, as fans of his aerial adventures may have heard, he earned his wings as a pioneering barnstormer at the dawn of American aviation. He also earned a place in free-flight record books for the longest sustained flight above Chicago. Moreover, as a roving reporter for *Sportsman Pilot* (featuring his first professionally penned articles), he further helped inspire a generation of pilots who would take America to world airpower.

Immediately beyond his sophomore year, Ron embarked on the first of his famed ethnological expeditions, initially to then untrammeled Caribbean shores (descriptions of which would later fill a whole series of West Indies mystery-thrillers). That the Puerto Rican interior would also figure into the future of Ron Hubbard stories was likewise no accident. For in addition to cultural studies of the island, a 1932–33

LRH expedition is rightly remembered as conducting the first complete mineralogical survey of a Puerto Rico under United States jurisdiction.

There was many another adventure along this vein: As a lifetime member of the famed Explorers Club, L. Ron Hubbard charted North Pacific waters with the first shipboard radio direction finder, and so pioneered a long-range navigation system universally employed until the late twentieth century. While not to put too fine an edge on it, he also held a rare Master Mariner's license to pilot any vessel, of any tonnage in any ocean.

Yet lest we stray too far afield, there is an LRH note at this juncture in his saga, and it reads in part:

"I started out writing for the pulps, writing the best I knew, writing for every mag on the stands, slanting as well as I could."

To which one might add: His earliest submissions date from the summer of 1934, and included tales drawn from true-to-life Asian adventures, with characters roughly modeled on British/American intelligence operatives he had known in Shanghai. His early Westerns were similarly peppered with details drawn from personal experience. Although therein lay a first hard lesson from the often cruel world of the pulps. His first Westerns were soundly rejected as lacking the authenticity of a Max Brand yarn

Capt. L. Ron Hubbard in Ketchikan, Alaska, 1940, on his Alaskan Radio Experimental Expedition, the first of three voyages conducted under the Explorers Club flag.

(a particularly frustrating comment given L. Ron Hubbard's Westerns came straight from his Montana homeland, while Max Brand was a mediocre New York poet named Frederick Schiller Faust, who turned out implausible six-shooter tales from the terrace of an Italian villa).

Nevertheless, and needless to say, L. Ron Hubbard persevered and soon earned a reputation as among the most publishable names in pulp fiction, with a ninety percent placement rate of first-draft manuscripts. He was also among the most prolific, averaging between seventy and a hundred thousand words a month. Hence the rumors that L. Ron Hubbard had redesigned a typewriter for faster keyboard action and pounded out manuscripts on a continuous roll of butcher paper to save the precious seconds it took to insert a single sheet of paper into manual typewriters of the day.

That all L. Ron Hubbard stories did not run beneath said byline is yet another aspect of pulp fiction lore. That is, as publishers periodically rejected manuscripts from top-drawer authors if only to avoid paying top dollar, L. Ron Hubbard and company just as frequently replied with submissions under various pseudonyms. In Ron's case, the list

A Man of Many Names

Between 1934 and 1950, L. Ron Hubbard authored more than fifteen million words of fiction in more than two hundred classic publications. To supply his fans and editors with stories across an array of genres and pulp titles, he adopted fifteen pseudonyms in addition to his already renowned L. Ron Hubbard byline.

Winchester Remington Colt
Lt. Jonathan Daly
Capt. Charles Gordon
Capt. L. Ron Hubbard
Bernard Hubbel
Michael Keith
Rene Lafayette
Legionnaire 148
Legionnaire 14830
Ken Martin
Scott Morgan
Lt. Scott Morgan
Kurt von Rachen
Barry Randolph
Capt. Humbert Reynolds

included: Rene Lafayette, Captain Charles Gordon, Lt. Scott Morgan and the notorious Kurt von Rachen—supposedly on the lam for a murder rap, while hammering out two-fisted prose in Argentina. The point: While L. Ron Hubbard as Ken Martin spun stories of Southeast Asian intrigue, LRH as Barry Randolph authored tales of romance on the Western range—which, stretching between a dozen genres is how he came to stand among the two hundred elite authors providing close to a million tales through the glory days of American Pulp Fiction.

L. Ron Hubbard, circa 1930, at the outset of a literary career that would finally span half a century.

In evidence of exactly that, by 1936 L. Ron Hubbard was literally leading pulp fiction's elite as president of New York's American Fiction Guild. Members included a veritable pulp hall of fame: Lester "Doc Savage" Dent, Walter "The Shadow" Gibson, and the legendary Dashiell Hammett—to cite but a few.

Also in evidence of just where L. Ron Hubbard stood within his first two years on the American pulp circuit: By the spring of 1937, he was ensconced in Hollywood, adopting a Caribbean thriller for Columbia Pictures, remembered today as *The Secret of Treasure Island.* Comprising fifteen thirty-minute episodes, the L. Ron Hubbard screenplay led to the most profitable matinée serial in Hollywood history. In accord with Hollywood culture, he was thereafter continually called

The 1937 Secret of Treasure Island, *a fifteen-episode serial adapted for the screen by L. Ron Hubbard from his novel,* Murder at Pirate Castle.

upon to rewrite/doctor scripts—most famously for long-time friend and fellow adventurer Clark Gable.

In the interim—and herein lies another distinctive chapter of the L. Ron Hubbard story—he continually worked to open Pulp Kingdom gates to up-and-coming authors. Or, for that matter, anyone who wished to write. It was a fairly unconventional stance, as markets were already thin and competition razor sharp. But the fact remains, it was an L. Ron Hubbard hallmark that he vehemently lobbied on behalf of young authors—regularly supplying instructional articles to trade journals, guest-lecturing to short story classes at George Washington University and Harvard, and even founding his own creative writing competition. It was established in 1940, dubbed the Golden Pen, and guaranteed winners both New York representation and publication in *Argosy.*

But it was John W. Campbell Jr.'s *Astounding Science Fiction* that finally proved the most memorable LRH vehicle. While every fan of L. Ron Hubbard's galactic epics undoubtedly knows the story, it nonetheless bears repeating: By late 1938, the pulp publishing magnate of Street & Smith was determined to revamp *Astounding Science Fiction* for broader readership. In particular, senior editorial director F. Orlin Tremaine called for stories with a stronger *human element.* When acting editor John W. Campbell balked, preferring his spaceship-driven tales,

Tremaine enlisted Hubbard. Hubbard, in turn, replied with the genre's first truly *character-driven* works, wherein heroes are pitted not against bug-eyed monsters but the mystery and majesty of deep space itself—and thus was launched the Golden Age of Science Fiction.

The names alone are enough to quicken the pulse of any science fiction aficionado, including LRH friend and protégé, Robert Heinlein, Isaac Asimov, A. E. van Vogt and Ray Bradbury. Moreover, when coupled with LRH stories of fantasy, we further come to what's rightly been described as the foundation of every modern tale of horror: L. Ron Hubbard's immortal Fear. It was rightly proclaimed by Stephen King as one of the very few works to genuinely warrant that overworked term "classic"—as in: *"This is a classic tale of creeping, surreal menace and horror. . . . This is one of the really, really good ones."*

L. Ron Hubbard, 1948, among fellow science fiction luminaries at the World Science Fiction Convention in Toronto.

To accommodate the greater body of L. Ron Hubbard fantasies, Street & Smith inaugurated *Unknown*—a classic pulp if there ever was one, and wherein readers were soon thrilling to the likes of *Typewriter in the Sky* and *Slaves of Sleep* of which Frederik Pohl would declare: *"There are bits and pieces from Ron's work that became part of the language in ways that very few other writers managed."*

And, indeed, at J. W. Campbell Jr.'s insistence, Ron was regularly drawing on themes from the Arabian Nights and so introducing readers to a world of genies, jinn, Aladdin and Sinbad—all of which, of course, continue to float through cultural mythology to this day.

At least as influential in terms of post-apocalypse stories was L. Ron Hubbard's 1940 *Final Blackout*. Generally acclaimed as the finest anti-war novel of the decade and among the ten best works of the genre ever authored—here, too, was a tale that would live on in ways few other writers imagined. Hence, the later Robert Heinlein verdict: "Final Blackout *is as perfect a piece of science fiction as has ever been written.*"

Portland, Oregon, 1943; L. Ron Hubbard captain of the US Navy subchaser PC 815.

Like many another who both lived and wrote American pulp adventure, the war proved a tragic end to Ron's sojourn in the pulps. He served with distinction in four theaters and was highly decorated for commanding corvettes in the North Pacific. He was also grievously wounded in combat, lost many a close friend and colleague and thus resolved to say farewell to pulp fiction and devote himself to what it had supported these many years—namely, his serious research.

But in no way was the LRH literary saga at an end, for as he wrote some thirty years later, in 1980:

"Recently there came a period when I had little to do. This was novel in a life so crammed with busy years, and I decided to amuse myself by writing a novel that was pure science fiction."

That work was *Battlefield Earth: A Saga of the Year 3000.* It was an immediate *New York Times* bestseller and, in fact, the first international science fiction blockbuster in decades. It was not, however, L. Ron Hubbard's magnum opus, as that distinction is generally reserved for his next and final work: The 1.2 million word *Mission Earth.*

Final Blackout ***is as perfect a piece of science fiction as has ever been written.***

—Robert Heinlein

How he managed those 1.2 million words in just over twelve months is yet another piece of the L. Ron Hubbard legend. But the fact remains, he did indeed author a ten-volume *dekalogy* that lives in publishing history for the fact that each and every volume of the series was also a *New York Times* bestseller.

Moreover, as subsequent generations discovered L. Ron Hubbard through republished works and novelizations of his screenplays, the mere fact of his name on a cover signaled an international bestseller. . . . Until, to date, sales of his works exceed hundreds of millions, and he otherwise remains among the most enduring and widely read authors in literary history. Although as a final word on the tales of L. Ron Hubbard, perhaps it's enough to simply reiterate what editors told readers in the glory days of American Pulp Fiction:

He writes the way he does, brothers, because he's been there, seen it and done it!

THE STORIES FROM THE GOLDEN AGE

Your ticket to adventure starts here with the Stories from the Golden Age collection by master storyteller L. Ron Hubbard. These gripping tales are set in a kaleidoscope of exotic locales and brim with fascinating characters, including some of the most vile villains, dangerous dames and brazen heroes you'll ever get to meet.

The entire collection of over one hundred and fifty stories is being released in a series of eighty books and audiobooks. For an up-to-date listing of available titles, go to www.goldenagestories.com.

AIR ADVENTURE

Arctic Wings
The Battling Pilot
Boomerang Bomber
The Crate Killer
The Dive Bomber
Forbidden Gold
Hurtling Wings
The Lieutenant Takes the Sky
Man-Killers of the Air
On Blazing Wings
Red Death Over China
Sabotage in the Sky
Sky Birds Dare!
The Sky-Crasher
Trouble on His Wings
Wings Over Ethiopia

FAR-FLUNG ADVENTURE

The Adventure of "X"
All Frontiers Are Jealous
The Barbarians
The Black Sultan
Black Towers to Danger
The Bold Dare All
Buckley Plays a Hunch
The Cossack
Destiny's Drum
Escape for Three
Fifty-Fifty O'Brien
The Headhunters
Hell's Legionnaire
He Walked to War
Hostage to Death
Hurricane
The Iron Duke
Machine Gun 21,000
Medals for Mahoney
Price of a Hat
Red Sand
The Sky Devil
The Small Boss of Nunaloha
The Squad That Never Came Back
Starch and Stripes
Tomb of the Ten Thousand Dead
Trick Soldier
While Bugles Blow!
Yukon Madness

SEA ADVENTURE

Cargo of Coffins
The Drowned City
False Cargo
Grounded
Loot of the Shanung
Mister Tidwell, Gunner
The Phantom Patrol
Sea Fangs
Submarine
Twenty Fathoms Down
Under the Black Ensign

TALES FROM THE ORIENT

The Devil—With Wings
The Falcon Killer
Five Mex for a Million
Golden Hell
The Green God
Hurricane's Roar
Inky Odds
Orders Is Orders
Pearl Pirate
The Red Dragon
Spy Killer
Tah
The Trail of the Red Diamonds
Wind-Gone-Mad
Yellow Loot

MYSTERY

The Blow Torch Murder
Brass Keys to Murder
Calling Squad Cars!
The Carnival of Death
The Chee-Chalker
Dead Men Kill
The Death Flyer
Flame City
The Grease Spot
Killer Ape
Killer's Law
The Mad Dog Murder
Mouthpiece
Murder Afloat
The Slickers
They Killed Him Dead

FANTASY

Borrowed Glory
The Crossroads
Danger in the Dark
The Devil's Rescue
He Didn't Like Cats
If I Were You
The Last Drop
The Room
The Tramp

SCIENCE FICTION

The Automagic Horse
Battle of Wizards
Battling Bolto
The Beast
Beyond All Weapons
A Can of Vacuum
The Conroy Diary
The Dangerous Dimension
Final Enemy
The Great Secret
Greed
The Invaders
A Matter of Matter
The Obsolete Weapon
One Was Stubborn
The Planet Makers
The Professor Was a Thief
The Slaver
Space Can
Strain
Tough Old Man
240,000 Miles Straight Up
When Shadows Fall

WESTERN

The Baron of Coyote River
Blood on His Spurs
Boss of the Lazy B
Branded Outlaw
Cattle King for a Day
Come and Get It
Death Waits at Sundown
Devil's Manhunt
The Ghost Town Gun-Ghost
Gun Boss of Tumbleweed
Gunman!
Gunman's Tally
The Gunner from Gehenna
Hoss Tamer
Johnny, the Town Tamer
King of the Gunmen
The Magic Quirt
Man for Breakfast
The No-Gun Gunhawk
The No-Gun Man
The Ranch That No One Would Buy
Reign of the Gila Monster
Ride 'Em, Cowboy
Ruin at Rio Piedras
Shadows from Boot Hill
Silent Pards
Six-Gun Caballero
Stacked Bullets
Stranger in Town
Tinhorn's Daughter
The Toughest Ranger
Under the Diehard Brand
Vengeance Is Mine!
When Gilhooly Was in Flower